Capital Strings

Teresa LaBella

This is an imprint of 4Wurdz Publishing

Caledonia, Nova Scotia. Canada

Author's Web site www.storyteller30.com

4Wurdz Press www.4wurdz.com

I ended the call and grabbed my coat. "J-lynn's car won't start."

"Can I help?"

"It probably just needs a jump." My phone chimed an incoming text message alert. "Maybe she's already got help." My wife was in the photo attached to the text message. But the image of her getting in her car wasn't taken in the nearby parking lot. "That's our townhouse!"

Colin leaned over my shoulder and read the message. "Seven ten."

"That's when she leaves for work." J-lynn walked toward the West Block in the next photo. The text read 7:25. Then the video app flickered on. My wife stood next to her car in fading daylight. She kicked at the driver's side door lock with the heel of her boot. "That bastard is in our back yard! Colin!"

"I'm on it." My second in command relayed orders alerting every RCMP officer, plainclothes security and guard on The Hill. We ran down stairs, hallways and through doors into the cold reality of snow-dusted concrete and possible ambush.

"Where's the prime minister?" I shouted over my shoulder.

"Still in his office."

"Tell his detail to keep him there!"

"Done."

I redialed the most important contact in my life. "Jerilynn! Get in your car. Lock the doors!"

"Alec? What's wrong?"

"Do it!"

Men and women in uniforms detained and hustled staff and visitors indoors and took positions in the parking lot. I knew more would surround The Hill perimeter. My jurisdiction was secure. But bullets don't respect boundaries. *You've made this personal, dickhead*, I screamed in my head. *Hunting you down is now my job one.*

To all the victims of gun violence and the advocates for gun control who are their voice.

Chapter 1

November 2022

Tires on three utility vehicles mulched the red, gold and brown remains of autumn. A spindled canopy of barren trees arched above an unpaved road. Clouds hid whatever warmth the sun tried to provide. Nature held its breath and waited for rain, ice or the season's first snowfall dependent on the timing of the advancing chill and overhead release on the forest, the lake and the cottage prepared for Canadian winter.

The late model gunmetal grey extended cab pickup disgorged a human bear of a man covered in layers of fleece and wool. Tall and strong with thighs thick as mature pine tree trunks and hands the size of dinner plates. Thick soles on his insulated boots crunched over loose gravel. A key from the ring crowded with others turned in the lock on the door not opened since August. Hinges creaked. The big man brushed the remnants of torn cobwebs from his beard and the brim of his cap and closed the door against the gathering gloom and increasing cold.

Outside, a Jeep wrapped in exterior camouflage and an aging Land Rover bearing the scars of off-road excursions ground to a stop. A middle-aged man with muscles forged and bulked by rigorous cross-fit training got out of the Land Rover and nodded to the woman in the Jeep. She slammed the driver's side door, zipped up her down jacket, and flipped a long braided ash blonde ponytail over her shoulder onto her back.

The new arrivals crossed into the cottage as flames from the fire set in the wood stove leaped to crackling life. A kerosene lamp at the center of the rough maple wood rectangular table cast shadows on the slatted plank wooden walls. The big man swung his legs over and sat on the bench tucked under the long side of the table. The muscled man and woman with the thick braid followed his lead on the opposite side bench.

"Where is the Ottawa contact?" the muscled man asked.

"He'll be here." The big man reached in the pocket of his vest. He offered a cigarette from the pack in his hand. Both refused. A match was struck. The end of the lit cigarette glowed in the dim light of a cottage with boarded up windows.

The crunch of tires on gravel and the rev of a twin-turbo V8 engine announced the presence of the last expected guest. The big man snuffed out the stub of cigarette in a metal bowl that rust had robbed of color. He got up and opened the door for the inches shorter and much thinner man in a black wool topcoat. White ice pellets slid through and melted in the strands of his slicked-back black hair. He entered and stomped his feet to dislodge damp debris stuck to his polished black leather boots.

"Excellent location," he said to the big man, "although a bit difficult to find even with the GPS." He strode past his host and stood at the end of the table. "Given the cold and threat of snow, let's make this brief, shall we." He slid the case in his hand onto the table and clicked open gold latches with his thumbs. "What is the status of the network?"

The big man grumbled an indecipherable response, tossed kindling on the fire, and returned to his place on the bench. "The network is up," he said. "We're ready."

"How extensive is its reach?" The man in the topcoat nudged black-rimmed glasses with thick corrective lenses up the bridge of his nose.

The muscled man unbuttoned the cuffs of his flannel shirt and shoved the sleeves half way up his forearms and over exposed paramilitary tattoos. "Every provincial capital from B.C. to Ontario and a few towns in between."

"How many?"

"Four in each location," replied the woman.

"No names?"

She shook her head. "Only location designations by code."

"Perfect." Topcoat man opened the case and handed a single sheet of paper to each of the three at the table. "This is a copy of the proposed amendment to the gun control law that will be read and entered in first reading next week."

Muscled man's face flamed red. "What the fuck is this shit?" His fist slammed the table. "I thought banning handguns was gonna be left up to city councils."

"Are we reading this right?" The woman squinted and frowned at the printed page in her hand. "Sale and ownership of handguns would be illegal in all of Canada?"

"That's correct." The contact from the capital of federal government removed the latest edition of The Globe and Mail from his case. The pile of folded newsprint plopped on the table chronicled the news for Sunday the 20th of November in the waning days of 2022. "Reporting in print on parliamentary procedure is more accurate than biased online and broadcast speculation. I brought you what I have. What you and your network choose to do with this information is entirely up to you. I can and will arrange monetary support for your endeavors." He closed the case and lifted it back into his hands. "Have a good evening."

The front door opened. A mix of ice pellets and snow skidded and sank into the rough grooves and cracked edges of the floor's boards. The sound of his vehicle's engine on the other side of the closed door revved and faded with distance. Fire in the woodstove flared, spit and crackled. The woman picked up the newspaper. Her eyes scanned the copy. "First automatic weapons were banned. Now this." She dropped the paper back on the table. "We can't let this happen."

"So what are we gonna do about it?" muscled man asked.

"Only one thing to do." Big man stood. "We need a change in government." He pointed his finger at the face in the photo on the front page above the fold and cocked his thumb in mock firing of a gun.

Chapter 2

New Year's Eve ~ Jerilynn

A layer of blankets over cotton sheets, a plump down duvet covered in woven flannel, fluffy pillows and a hot cup of coffee brought to me by the sexiest man alive who also happens to be my husband.

What could top that? I thought.

"A day away from Parliament Hill." I stretched from my covered toes to the tips of my fingers. Nature's frosting on the windows forecast a cold and snowy New Year's Eve.

"Happy anniversary, gorgeous." Alec's kisses stoke my fire every time our lips meet and our tongues touch. "It's a toss-up which is hotter – what's in the cup or between the sheets."

I took the cup from him, sipped milky foam from the rim, and licked my lips. "Delicious." I folded back the layers that warmed my naked skin and patted the mattress.

The heat in his milk chocolate brown eyes rose with his smile. "What about your coffee?" He took the cup from my hands and set it on the bedside table.

"You can pour me a fresh cup. I don't like it cold."

The ruby red robe I'd given him for Christmas fell open to nothing underneath. His body on mine and our lively romp of passion to pleasure raised the temperature between us by several degrees Celsius.

"J-lynn." Alec breathed his pet name for me in the afterglow tease of my fingernails through the dark hair on his chest and sensual points down below. "I could spend every minute of our day right here."

I snuggled closer and covered us with the mound of bed clothes. "While that has its appeal, we should think about having breakfast."

His eyelids snapped open. "Oh shit! The scones!" My amateur chef in charge of the kitchen when he was not in command of the Parliamentary Protective Service bolted from our bed and down the stairs of our townhouse. I giggled when the smoke detector shrieked. Ten minutes later, Alec returned with a tray of salvaged sweet and savory scones, a bowl of fresh fruit, and two steamy cups of fresh coffee.

"So, my love," Alec said. "How are we going to celebrate seven years of fantastic sex and marital bliss?" He unpeeled a banana and offered me the first bite. The suggestive gesture for more of the former was not lost on me.

"As much as I would love to test the limits of your prowess, we do have to make an appearance at Rideau Cottage this evening."

An unintelligible but clear message of protest escaped over his mouthful of cinnamon raisin scone washed down with coffee. "I don't suppose there's any graceful way out of that."

"No, there is not. The prime minister is my boss, I'm his chief of staff and your job exists in large part because you protect him."

"Those are three good reasons."

"Three very good reasons." I finished my cheddar scone and swallowed the last of the coffee in my cup. "He knows it's our anniversary. He'll thank us for coming and graciously ease our exit."

"OK. You're right. We'll be politically correct and go to the PM's soiree." Alec piled the empty plates and cups on the tray and carried the remains of breakfast downstairs.

We need to talk about where we go from here, Alec. The federal election in October could mean the end of my dream job. My boss might decide he's had enough of Liberal Party leadership. I wouldn't be surprised if he does. Our first four years were rough enough. Every bill passed in the House of Commons to restore programs gutted by eight years of Conservative government budget cuts was a battle even with a majority government. Mudslinging during the campaign leading up to the 2019 election hurled accusations from sources the opposition ignored but also declined to denounce. Words like 'traitor' and 'treason' aimed at the prime minister after debates on laws banning the ownership and sale of assault weapons and handguns.

Waves of contagion spread in 2020 and stress levels soared with the urgency to keep Canadians safe until everyone who wanted one got vaccinated. Rebuilding the damaged economy continues to be a burden. The big question now is who will step up if my boss steps down? The deputy prime minister has made it clear that she has no interest in the top job. Rumor has it the PM's public safety minister and a Member of Parliament from our home province of Nova Scotia will likely get the party's vote of confidence. Alec's job on Parliament Hill is up to the whim of the RCMP Commissioner and the speakers of the House and Senate. I'm not too concerned about my career. In politics and business, it's all about who you know. But the job and title I want most is not entirely up to me and apparently out of my control.

I've blown off two scheduled appointments at the OB/GYN in the past six months. Even without the shots to prevent pregnancy, those familiar cramps return with that regular monthly cycle. I haven't told Alec. In fact, we've never talked about it. We were too busy competing for valedictorian as high school sweethearts to concentrate on anything but our career ambitions. Since we met up again and got married six weeks later, having a family has never been discussed. I want a baby, Alec. But I'm not sure if you do.

He came back with a dozen red and white roses wrapped in cellophane and tied with red ribbon. I cradled the fragrant bundle and sniffed the delicate petals. "They're beautiful," I said.

"So are you." His soft kiss reminded me of the first so long ago, our junior year in high school, before we grew up, lost touch, and found each other again. The kiss deepened and rekindled my fire. "These need water," I whispered.

He took the roses from my arms. "I need you."

We made love under blanketed warmth as the snow fell on Ottawa the last day of 2022.

Chapter 3

Alec

Rank has its privileges, especially when entering the fortified perimeter of security that Rideau Hall Grounds has unfortunately become.

Off limits to the general public when the governor general and the prime minister are in residence. Restricted by invitation or scheduled pre-screened tours even when they're not. All thanks to an angry man with a stockpile of illegal weapons and a grudge against government in the peak of a pandemic.

"Good evening, sir." The uniformed RCMP sentinel on duty at 1 Sussex Drive scanned my ID. Reinforced towering black wrought iron gates opened with buzz click recognition. Snow swirled in the headlights required to navigate December darkness. Lights in the windows, on the porch and along the pathway of Rideau Cottage shone like beacons of celebration up ahead.

I handed over the car keys to a uniformed valet and opened the passenger side door for my radiant life partner. "Blue becomes you, my love," I commented on the color of the moonlit midnight dress she'd chosen for the occasion, "but considering the season and the political party you represent, maybe you should have worn that sexy red dress."

"Red makes me look like a cupcake with vanilla icing." She patted thick past shoulder-length white-blond hair tamed by deep blue cloisonné enamel combs. My arm around the petite powerhouse I'd married steadied her on three inch heels. The top of her head was just level with my shoulder.

A rush of warmth, hired help offers to take our coats and enjoy a glass of champagne, and Angeline Reid welcomed us on the other side of the front door. My first and lasting impression of her can best be described as the opposite of J-lynn. Where my wife is an M&M, tough on the outside but melts when her thick shell is cracked, the prime minister's wife presents as a delicate beauty with a porcelain fragile personality underneath. Soft spoken and satisfied to stay in her husband's shadow. Yet I've always sensed an inner strength from her that could defy and defeat any opposition.

"Jerilynn." She hugged my wife, stepped back and touched the sleeve of my jacket at the elbow. "Happy anniversary."

"Thank you," we said.

"How many years has it been?"

"Seven," I replied.

"Oh, yes I remember. You met the day after Evan was sworn in."

"Well, it's more accurate to say we reconnected," my wife replied.

We heard her boss before we saw him and the conversation had nothing to do with politics.

"Either choose another movie or go to bed."

"But Dad." A prepubescent male in a nearby room raised his voice in protest and volume over the ambient chatter of guests. "We just watched 'The Sound of Music' and it was boring."

"We're not tired," another child complained in a distinct little girl whine. "Can we sing a song like the kids in the movie did?"

"Can't I stay and taste my first champagne?" an older girl asked in a pitch and tone much like her mother's.

"We are not the von Trapp family. Upstairs. Now."

"Excuse me." Angeline left us to mingle on our own among Liberal Party Members of Parliament from ridings in and around Ottawa, other guests I didn't recognize, and RCMP Commissioner Christine Burke. Governor General Francine Deveraux was in her element, spreading smiles and a reminder invitation to the New Year's Day levee at her Rideau Hall residence.

I lowered my voice and lips to J-lynn's ear. "We don't have to go to that too, do we?"

"No, we're not that far up in the high society food chain," she said.

A man of average height, round in the middle and bald under the obvious comb over, loudly apologized for bouncing his well-fed middle off the hip of a tall woman in a gold satin dress fit snug to hold every curve. His clumsy advance through the guests appeared to be on a course to intercept us.

"Uh-oh." Jerilynn glanced in his direction and turned away.

"I take it you know who that is."

"Vincent Lockwood. Ottawa South riding back bencher. He's exhausting. Talks without taking a breath."

"Well, hello!" MP Apple Belly circled around and in front of us. "I was hoping I'd see you here. You look stunning, Ms. Connor." J-lynn backed away from his attempt to kiss her cheek. She took his hand instead. He stuck the same hand out toward me. "And you must be Chief Superintendent Martin." His breath reeked of garlic and bourbon. I shook his hand and maintained my distance. "So, I'd like to know what the two of you think of the amendment to Bill C-71. I'm especially interested in your opinion as an officer of the law."

"Excuse me?" I asked.

"The amendment to the gun control bill that will make owning a handgun illegal in Canada." He leaned in so close that I could have unclipped his crooked red bow tie with my teeth. "Do we really need that extra layer of enforcement? The laws on handgun ownership and transport in Canada are already quite restrictive, especially when compared to our American neighbors."

"I'm not at liberty to comment."

"Why not? How can that law be enforced if the amendment becomes law? The RCMP will have to solve that problem. How can we keep handguns that are now illegal from coming into the country without significantly beefing up the border patrol?"

"Parliament Hill is my only jurisdiction. All weapons are illegal within the boundaries of the Parliamentary precinct."

"I'm aware of that. I was on the committee that supported the bill and set up the protective service. But you are an RCMP officer and the RCMP will bear the brunt of enforcing the amended gun control law."

Idle chatter from the turned heads around us stopped. This game of verbal volleyball was attracting too many spectators. My wife charged the net and spiked the ball.

"Mr. Lockwood, this is not the appropriate place for this discussion. You are welcome to present your concerns in my office after holiday break." She slipped her arm through mine. "Happy New Year to you." His chin continued to wag as we walked away.

"Is that guy always such a dickhead? Or was that a 'seize the opportunity' performance?" I asked her.

"Both. He's high on my keep this MP away from the PM list."

"Jerilynn!" An older woman, elegant in emerald green and a single strand of pearls, kissed my wife's cheek and embraced her like a daughter. The distinctive chestnut brown hair tone shared by her son identified Celine Reid, widow of Prime Minister Tony Reid and mother of the current holder of that right honourable title for life. "My goodness, you look so lovely, my dear."

"Thank you. Did you have a nice Christmas?"

"Oh, yes. I've been here with Evan and dear Angeline and my grandchildren since Christmas Eve. I had a wonderful long talk with Jonathan on Christmas Day. He's my son who lives in New Zealand. Have you met him?"

"No, I haven't," J-lynn replied.

"I didn't think you had. He doesn't come home very often. It is a long flight, you know. But I do miss him so very much. Evan would never admit it. But I think he misses his brother, too. They were always so close growing up. They loved to go fishing with their father. I could never understand why anyone would want to sit in a boat all day and get chewed up by black flies and mosquitoes and what have you. Sometimes they'd come back with nothing. But when they did, oh my." She pinched her nose and grimaced. "The smell! I made them clean those fish before they brought them home." She took a breath and turned to me. "Are you Jerilynn's husband? Have we met?"

"Yes to both questions, Mrs. Reid," I said. "Alec Martin."

"Oh, of course. You're the RCMP officer."

"He's Director of Parliamentary Protective Service, Mum."

Relief at last! The prime minister stood behind his mother. His hands rested easily on her shoulders.

"That's a big job," Celine said. "But I'm sure that you are more than qualified. How long have you been with the RCMP?"

The prime minister cut in. "Mum, it's their anniversary."

"Well, happy anniversary." She clasped our hands in hers. "Do you have children?"

Now that's a loaded question, I thought.

"No. We don't," was my wife's definitive answer.

Well, there it is. Short and not so sweet. Truth spoken and noted. Case closed.

"You should. Children are such a blessing." She sighed and shook her head. "Christmas isn't Christmas without children. Don't you think so, Evan?"

From the change in his usual game face for occasions, I got the feeling the prime minister had squared off with less aggressive opponents in the House of Commons. As the son of a mother with a similar talk-and-question-until-the-other-side-caves style, I understood his conflict.

"Mum. Would you go upstairs and make sure the children are in bed?"

"Of course I will, dear." She took a breath. I braced for another barrage. "Only Grandma knows how to properly tuck them in."

We all exhaled when she left the room.

"I'm sorry I couldn't come to your rescue sooner," the prime minister said.

"It's OK," Jerilynn reassured her boss. "Your mother is very sweet."

"And verbose."

I sensed he was about to offer the ease of exit plan mentioned earlier by my wife.

"I'm sure you have other plans. Please, if you're ready, let me walk you to the door."

We followed him through the clusters of guests to the front hallway. Coats retrieved, we prepared to leave.

He stuck out his hand. "Happy anniversary." As always, I was impressed at the strength of his grip.

"Happy New Year, boss." My wife reached up and gave him a quick hug. He whispered something in her ear and strode back into the fray.

On the drive home, I asked J-lynn what the prime minister had said to her. She didn't answer right away. "Look, I get it if it's none of my business or something I don't need to know."

"Don't be a jerk," she said.

I bristled when I shouldn't have. "Fine." Only the slap of windshield wipers against the steady fall of wet snow and an occasional honk from a car horn broke the silence.

We walked through our front door with thirty minutes left in the old year. I hung up our coats, flopped in my leather recliner, and tried to compose an apology and excuse for a stupid and baseless reaction. I am not jealous, I half-assed lied to myself. *He's the Prime Minister and her boss. But he's a man and some weeks he spends more waking hours with my wife than I do.*

J-lynn went upstairs. She returned a few minutes later with two glasses of champagne, wearing the fluffy pink robe I'd given her for Christmas. She handed me a glass, sat on my lap, and opened the robe. To my delight, she wore nothing underneath.

I forgot the excuse.

"Happy New Year, my love," she said.

We clicked our glasses and drank to us. My hand between her thighs got us both ready to celebrate the arrival of 2023.

Chapter 4

January 2023 ~ Evan

Cabinet ministers required for the first line of discussion on the final amendment to Bill C-71 responded to my call to arms meeting two weeks before Parliament's return to the House of Commons. We gathered around the table reserved for the Liberal Party caucus in the West Block where cleaners would outnumber Parliament Hill staff for a few more days.

Deputy Prime Minister Carla Mendez, the reluctant rising star in the Liberal Party, had made it clear to the party caucus that she did not want my job and no amount of persuasion would alter that irrevocable decision. "I'll let you know when I've had enough," she'd told me the day my office announced the elevated change of her position in my cabinet from Minister of Economic Development. "And you'd best let me know when you have. I've got a business, a husband and two daughters waiting for me in Vancouver where the air is cleaner and the mountains we climb are real."

Finance Minister Lee Mitchell possesses that rare combination of personable numbers cruncher. I've never encountered anyone else with the uncanny ability to accurately add, subtract, multiply and divide columns of numbers on paper without assistance from a device of any kind. I leaned heavily on the CPA and former professor of economics at the University of Toronto as our G7 economy without a budget rode out the pandemic-induced trillion dollar deficit tsunami. We're not back yet but Lee has kept us on track toward a full recovery.

Asad Bashir is the youngest Member of Parliament tapped to serve in a prime minister's cabinet as Leader of the Government in the House of Commons. He has the portfolio of a forty-year-old at the age of twenty-nine. Asad's long list of achievements began as Canada's top prize winning contestant of the National Spelling Bee in Washington D.C. at age nine. Top of class double major masters level graduate of the Massachusetts Institute of Technology in political science and linguistics, he returned home to Montreal after five years as a translator at the United Nations. In the next election he accomplished the impossible, winning the support of the Hassidic Jewish community as a Muslim in his Outremont riding.

Minister of Public Safety David Getti rose to public prominence as a tough but fair law enforcement officer for the Halifax Regional Police. His reputation for de-escalating sensitive situations and work as liaison with the Board of Police Commissioners earned him the respect of and eventual employment with the Halifax District RCMP, a place on the Nova Scotia Serious Incident Response Team, and rank of deputy commissioner prior to his election to Parliament. Our success in keeping as many Canadians safe as possible during the pandemic could be credited in large part to the MP from Halifax. Needless to say, his interest in doubling down on federal gun control increased after the April 2020 tragic rampage in his home province.

Hannah Jeffries was the clear and only choice for Minister of Justice and Attorney General. No one else in the history of Canada's court system had so successfully and eloquently represented clients, applied legislation in provincial and national jurisdictions and interpreted the Constitution and Canadian Charter of Rights and Freedoms, both as an attorney and Member of Parliament from Calgary. Her calm demeanor and subtle sense of humour keep us focused on the how and why we're all here.

"Thanks for cutting your time away a bit short," I said. "I want to take a hard look at where we're at on the Firearms Act amendments."

"Well, the regulatory work on tougher background checks that got held up by the pandemic is finally done." Dave Getti reached for the full carafe in the center of the table and poured himself a cup of coffee. "All that's needed now is an order-in-council from cabinet."

"And the money to pay for it," Lee Mitchell responded. "It's there and ready to spend as soon as the budget is approved."

"What about funding for technology to track valid licenses before sales?" Dave continued. "And don't we need that technology for lifetime checks?" he asked. "I'm not sure that would have saved any lives in Nova Scotia but it might have reduced his stockpile," he said, referring to the gunman who killed twenty-two people before the RCMP shot and killed him.

"There's money in the budget for that as well," my finance minister confirmed.

"Parliament still needs to give the go ahead on the assault weapon buyback," Asad Bashir reminded us. "The opposition will no doubt try to use that as a bargaining chip or to pile on the rhetoric against the handgun ban, whether the $350 million to cover the cost of the buyback is in the budget or not."

"I do have concerns regarding the total ban of handguns," Hannah Jeffries said. "While it can be done legally as there is no constitutional right for gun ownership in Canada. Why change one plank of the supported election promise?"

"The attorney general has a good point," my DPM said. "Military-style assault weapons have been banned. Why is it not enough to allow cities to decide whether and how to ban handguns?"

"That's going to be a tough sell in Parliament," Asad agreed.

"Yes, it is." I leaned forward and made eye contact with each member of my cabinet around that table. "Since when have we backed away from challenging the opposition on an issue or a law that will protect Canadians? Gun homicides have more than doubled in five years. More than half of those victims died because someone had access to a handgun. Break and enter crimes to steal firearms have doubled. A third of the four thousand firearms reported stolen last year were handguns. Handguns and assault weapons are used for one purpose. To kill people. I told Canadians that there is no place in our country for military-style assault weapons. There is no reason why a person who is not in the military or law enforcement needs to own a handgun."

"I've been both military and police," Dave said. "I agree with the prime minister. Too many people licensed to own a handgun don't know how to use one. That's where the phrase 'shooting yourself in the foot' originated. Amateurs are a danger to themselves and others and that includes cops that have to confront some wannabe with a gun that gets in the way of a clear field to observe and fire."

"What about people who shoot handguns for sport?" Carla asked.

17

"I believe Minister Getti already answered that question," Hannah said. "If they are not legally licensed owners of handguns as members of the military or police, are they not by definition amateurs?"

Carla nodded. "I can't argue with that," she said.

"So, we go forward with Bill C-71 as amended." I stood to signal meeting adjourned. "On to second reading. Thank you, everyone. If not before, I'll see you in two weeks."

§

Who is Evan Reid? I ask myself that question every morning, before every briefing with the ministers in my cabinet, every sitting of the House of Commons, every news conference and meeting with the premiers of each and all ten provinces and three territories.

I am the husband of a woman as strong as she is beautiful. My Angeline, mother to the three most precious gifts of life and joy I could have dared hope for, put her own talents and ambitions on hold for mine.

I am the son of a great man who to me and my brother Jon was just Dad, whether he was introducing us to royalty or showing us how to properly clean a fish. I am the protector of my Mum, a gentle, fragile spirit that lost so much of its spark when Dad passed away. The fierce devotion of their love and respect for one another blazed until his fire went out.

I am a teacher eager to share what I've learned with the young people that are the future of our country and the world.

Who is Evan Reid? The answer that rarely comes to me is the most important to the most people. I am the first son to follow his father as the Right Honourable Prime Minister of Canada.

The second question I ask myself every morning is how the hell did THIS happen?

I don't remember much about my very early childhood in Victoria, the provincial capital of British Columbia. Dad was mayor, then an MP, and Leader of the Liberal Party in rapid succession. We moved to Ottawa when Dad became prime minister, before I started the public school my Mum insisted I attend. My classmates teased me about the RCMP car following the school bus.

The expectations began the day I graduated high school. Dad saw law school in my future. Mum encouraged me to be whatever and whoever I wanted to be. I listened to Mum, worked as a camp counselor in the summer, earned undergraduate and graduate degrees in education, and got my first job teaching English Language Arts and French to sixth graders in Saskatoon, Saskatchewan. Eight blissful years doing what I loved in a place where my family name and history really didn't matter so much.

A visit home during summer holiday changed everything. My brother introduced me to the woman I would marry then broke the news over beers and fishing rods of Dad's plans for our future. One of us had to carry on the family tradition in politics and it wasn't going to be Jon. "I can't see myself wearing a suit and tie, knowing what to say and when to keep my mouth shut. Can you?" I had to admit he was right. "Thanks, man," he said when I agreed to quit my job, move to Ottawa and run for MP in the liberal stronghold Ottawa-Vanier riding. "I owe you one." He'll never be able to pay me back.

After the shock of relocation, career reinvention and swapping single life for marriage and sleepless nights with a newborn wore off, the six years spent in the backbench of the House of Commons proved rewarding. I ignored the snide remarks from MPs who labeled me "Prince Privileged" and "the backbench oddity" and embraced the task of doing my job. I listened to the people's concerns in my riding, did my homework, asked questions and took pride in getting the answers. The Liberal Party took notice of my success at attaining consistently high approval ratings and winning elections by unprecedented percentages at a time when the party's recent overall record was not so good. I turned them down three times, once for each of our children, when asked to lead the Liberal Party. I wanted to be there for my son and daughter and the baby on the way as my father had not for me and my brother. My sigh of relief when New Brunswick MP Alan Beckett agreed to lead was short lived. With Beckett backing out due to personal health concerns and the 2015 election rapidly approaching, I couldn't say no again.

We campaigned on a message of sharing the wealth with every Canadian. The Liberal Party won a majority government. Just like that, I was sworn in as prime minister. But only for four years, I told Angeline. I'll go back to teaching, I promised my wife the day we brought our second baby girl home. No, you won't, she said, and she was right. Another election, another Liberal Party majority and four more years as prime minister, an honour and responsibility I could once again not refuse.

Before we could put together a budget and begin the work of keeping promises made during the hard fought 2019 campaign, a deadly pandemic upended our lives. The shelter in place, social distancing, wear a mask reality closed businesses, erased jobs and deflated our economy. I suffered with every one of the confirmed cases of the illness and mourned for the families of each of the dead.

In the midst of that unimaginable health threat, the unthinkable happened in Nova Scotia. A man resolved whatever his grudge was with the world by masquerading as an officer of the law and killing innocent people. While Parliament was meeting virtually due to the pandemic stay at home order, I followed through with the first part of a campaign promise and introduced a measure by order-in-council from cabinet that banned the possession and sale of assault-style weapons in Canada. Owners of these weapons had two years to turn them in to police, sell them to buyers outside Canada with a permit, or participate in a Canadian government buyback of the weapons without penalty or prosecution. Parliament has yet to approve the buyback option and the resulting one-year extension of the amnesty period is about to expire. What's next will likely further mobilize and entrench the opposition.

The second part of my government's gun control campaign promise gives municipalities the option to ban handguns within their boundaries. But what I intend to do with the amendment to the law entered on first reading in November is ban the sale and ownership of all firearms that have no purpose but to kill people.

This could be my last battle as prime minister. If it is, I will leave knowing I did my job. I kept Canadians safe.

Chapter 5

Willie

The highest defrost setting was no match for the layer of ice that coated the windshield of Willie Carlyle's older model olive green Buick sedan. He kicked at the pile of snow brushed from the car's windows and hood and cursed when a sudden gust of wind blew the powdery white stuff back in his face.

Willie yanked open the semi-frozen driver's side door, slid over the cracks in the cheap vinyl and slammed the door closed. Lukewarm air from the vehicle's vents flowed over his fingers, red from the cold and the fact he'd lost yet another pair of gloves. Willie watched the sky change from pre-dawn grey to the first light of dreary. When the ice had melted enough to clear the glass with wipers, the night security guard drove out of the parking lot and away from Parliament Hill.

Plows had scraped most of the snow from the streets between the only employer that would hire him and the home that wasn't. He checked the time on the dashboard clock. 7:15. If he drove a little slower, his father may have left for work and breakfast could be peaceful for a change. His sister would still be in bed. His niece would be on the bus headed for school. His mother would take her cup of tea onto the heated four season porch and sit on the red and white striped cushion in her white wicker chair next to the round glass-topped white wicker table. She'd reach for the radio on the table, turn on CBC News, and leave Willie alone in the kitchen with his bowl of corn flakes, two pieces of buttered white toast and the rest of the tea brewed in the white china pot with painted pink roses.

The mental image of quiet solitude before sleep dissolved in the exhaust from the black Mercedes backing out of the driveway of the detached house with a single-car garage. The only address Willie had ever had. *I can drive away. Circle the block. Maybe go to Timmy's and get a double-double.* Willie slowed his car, checked for traffic and swerved to avoid the rear bumper of his father's car.

The Mercedes' brake lights flashed. The driver's side door opened. "William!" His father shouted, emerged from the car, and slammed the door. Tan wool top coat over perfectly-pressed dark brown slacks. Brown leather gloves. Tan and brown plaid scarf tucked in a V under the coat's lapels and his clean-shaven cheeks and chin. Rubber boots zippered over the inevitable pair of impeccably shined wingtips. No hat. William Carlyle Senior rarely covered what he considered his salt-and-steel asset.

Willie backed the car to the curb and turned the key in the ignition. The car engine shuddered, wheezed and died. He got out of the car and trudged through salted street sludge to the snow-packed sidewalk.

"Where the hell do you think you're going?" his father demanded. "I almost didn't make it out of the garage. The snow shovel was not where it was supposed to be. Do you have any idea where it is?"

How the hell should I know? He thought but didn't dare say. "I'm not sure."

"Find it. I expect the walk to look like it would on a summer day when I come home from work. And don't forget the driveway. I plan to park in the garage tonight."

Willie shrugged shoulders hitched up to his ears by sore and always rigid muscles. "Anything else?"

"As a matter of fact there is. Your mother needs you to drive her to the store and the pharmacy. Fix the back door. It's about to fall off. And stop slouching!"

The Mercedes taillights flashed unlocked door acknowledgement. William "Bill" Carlyle, attorney at law and former Conservative Party Member of Parliament twice defeated, got in and drove away in newer model luxury. His son went to look for the snow shovel. The screen door opened as he rounded the west side of the house.

"Willie?" Rose Carlyle held the metal door at arm's length. The solid wooden door at her back closed as tight as it could against the heels of her bedroom slippers. Willie noticed two screws were missing from the top hinge. "Come in and have your breakfast. I've laid the table and the tea is getting cold."

"Have you seen the snow shovel? I could have sworn I left it on the front porch."

"Don't worry about that now. CBC Radio says there's more snow on the way. Come inside and have something to eat."

"Alright, Mom." Willie followed her in and took off his coat. He kicked off his boots on the braided rug inside the door and padded on stocking feet across the linoleum. His sister seated at the kitchen table startled him.

"What?" Annabel asked through a mouthful of corn flakes and milk. "I live here, too, remember? If you can call this living."

We both know it isn't. Hasn't been and never will be. "I thought you'd still be asleep."

"I wish I were. But the old man was in top form this morning. He's been preaching the gospel of 'I hate Evan Reid' since five-thirty. I drove Fiona to school to get away from it."

"Not sorry I missed that." Willie hung up his coat in the hallway closet and sat across the table from his sister. He poured tea from the china pot into the brown mug on the edge of the laminated souvenir place mat from the Toronto Zoo and wrapped his hands around the mug. The warmth of the tea within soothed his inner chill.

"Would you like me to make you some oatmeal, Willie?" his mother asked.

"Hey! Why does he rate cooked cereal and I don't?" Annabel whined.

"Because he just got off work, he's cold, and you won't eat oatmeal," Rose told her daughter.

"That would be great, Mom, thank you," Willie said.

The radio on the other side of the open French doors to the sun porch played louder than usual this morning. Rose hummed along with the broadcast tune while she stirred oatmeal into water boiling in a pot on the stove.

"So how is little Miss Fiona?" Willie asked his sister. "I don't think I've seen her since Christmas break."

"She's busy."

"Doing what?"

"Being thirteen."

"That's not telling me much. What's the big secret?"

"No big secret. Fiona hates being here almost as much as I do." She glanced up at her brother. "As we do."

Willie's grip tightened around the mug. "I'm making enough money to move out."

"So why don't you?"

He squinted at his sister through bloodshot eyes. "I stay for you and Fiona and Mom. I hate to think what that bastard would do if I left. Or if we left him all alone with her."

Rose brought the pot from stove to table and plopped breakfast into Willie's bowl. "Are you going in to work today?" she asked Annabel.

"My first appointment is booked at one. A repeat client who always tips big. Full body massage, manicure and pedicure. Ka-ching!" Annabel framed her face with her open hands, palms forward and fingers spread for visual effect.

"So you won't be picking Fiona up from school?" Rose asked.

"No. She can ride the bus home."

"We can pick her up after I take you to the store, Mom," Willie volunteered. "Dad said you need to go to the pharmacy, too."

"Oh, Willie, don't worry about that. I can take something out of the freezer for dinner. You need your sleep."

"It's no big deal. I'll take a nap and then we can go." *I only sleep a couple of hours anyway*, he thought but would never tell her. *I stay in my room and play games on my smartphone so you think I'm sleeping and won't worry so much.*

"Annabel, do you know if Fiona will be home for dinner tonight?"

"I doubt it. I think she's totally fed up listening to Dad's nightly anti-liberal rants. Now he's started revving that engine in the morning." Annabel sighed and looked up at her mother. "Mom, can't you get him to lighten up?"

"Oh, you're exaggerating."

"No, she's not, Mom," Willie said. "Dad gets red-faced every night over dinner. Tells us how much he hates contract law. How much he loved the House of Commons. That he'd still be an MP if it wasn't for 'Prince Privileged'. That the prime minister ruined his life. That he's ruined ours."

"Yeah, about that." Annabel got up and stacked her dirty dishes in the sink. "Who exactly is responsible for ruining our lives? Dad? The prime minister? Or have we done that all by ourselves?"

"Annabel. Please." Rose cupped her hands over her ears.

"Look at us, Mom! Open your eyes! You sit around all day in your bathrobe and slippers. I give massages and paint the fingernails and toenails of people with too much time and money on their hands. Willie stays up all night five nights a week roaming the halls on Parliament Hill. And my daughter without a father doesn't want to sit around this table and have dinner with her miserable grandfather

26

who hates a guy because his name and who he is got him elected when our old man couldn't."

CBC Radio news filled the moments of no response. "On Parliament Hill, Prime Minister Evan Reid announced his government's intention to move forward on an amendment to the gun control law that will make handgun sales and ownership illegal in all of Canada."

"Great." Willie went to the sink and ran water over the dirty dishes. "Now we know the topic of tonight's gospel of 'I hate Evan Reid'." He unbuttoned the cuffs on the sleeves of his shirt with uniform patches. "I'm going to bed."

Chapter 6

The Official Opposition

The hard soles of black leather wingtips slapped in echoed rhythm across floors freshly polished over holiday break. The bell summoning parliamentarians to the House of Commons wouldn't ring for another six days.

Kingston Poirier wore a formal black suit and tie and white dress shirt to an informal meeting. The Conservative Member of Parliament and shadow minister of public safety strode past cleaners and security guards without acknowledging their work or presence in the West Block. The key in the lock opened his office. He noted the time on his cell phone. A finger tap summoned his parliamentary assistant.

"I'm at my office, Douglas. Be here in three minutes or I will begin the search for your replacement." He ended the call without waiting for a reply. The cell phone he discarded slid to stop on the smooth finish of a desk devoid of clutter.

Poirier positioned his briefcase on the desk and hung the black topcoat in the armoire he'd requisitioned. He frowned at the rapid rap of rubber-soled shoes in the hallway toward and through his office door. The digital read out on his wristwatch confirmed two minutes and forty seconds had passed since the cell phone call. "In under the wire again." The MP sat behind his desk and straightened his tie. Ice blue eyes enlarged by thick lenses scanned the younger man from the pale green shirt half-tucked into khakis to the laced-up hiking boots on his feet. "Inappropriate attire." He glared at the assistant assigned to him. "You are here to observe and take notes. Did you bring a notepad or must I supply you with that as well as a pen?"

"I have a pad and pen, sir." The required writing tools appeared in his hand, taken from the pocket of a navy blue wool pea coat. He sat in the chair to Poirier's left and waited for further instructions.

"Anybody home?" The overweight middle-aged man, casually dressed in jeans and a mustard yellow rag wool sweater, stood in the office doorway.

"Vincent." Poirier stood, smiled and greeted his colleague from the other side of the aisle. "Please. Come in." He turned to his assistant. "Close the door behind Mr. Lockwood." He crossed the room to a round conference table for four and rolled out a chair for the Liberal Party MP. "Thank you so much for agreeing to meet at such an inconvenient time."

Lockwood chuckled and settled in the chair. "You know as well as I do holiday break doesn't start until Christmas Eve or last past Boxing Day. Places to go. People to see. Backs to pat, hands to shake and a shopping list of phone calls to make. No rest for saints, sinners or MPs. I warned my wife when I won my riding. This isn't a nine to five, weekends and holidays off job honey, I said. I told my kids 'Don't complain when Dad's not around'. They still do, though. Every time it's just Nancy in the bleachers or warming the seat at a recital." Lockwood tugged at the sleeves of his sweater and pulled the wool over the top of his beltless jeans. "Sorry. I didn't know this was an official meeting."

"It isn't."

Lockwood lifted his stubbled chin toward Douglas frantically scribbling on the notepad. "Then why is your assistant here?" He turned and glanced around the room. "Is anyone else from the committee coming?"

"No, Vincent. I wanted to keep this discussion of the prime minister's amendment to the gun control bill as private as possible. Douglas is taking notes to refer to should that become necessary." Poirier sat facing Lockwood. "I've heard that you have misgivings about supporting your party and party leader on this issue."

"Well, I." Lockwood cleared his throat and picked at a mid-chest snag in his sweater. "I did object when the prime minister banned assault weapons by order-in-council from cabinet. I thought that should have been debated and voted on in the House of Commons."

"Yes, that is always the preferred course of action. Canadians expect that of their government. The prime minister violated that trust."

Lockwood shifted in his chair. "I wouldn't go that far. I may not support every decision he's made. He has his faults. But Evan Reid cares about Canadians. Our government with him at the helm got us through the pandemic. We're in a helluva lot better shape than our neighbors to the south because Canada had leadership when we really needed it. I'm proud of our government's record during that long and drawn out threat to life and livelihoods. The prime minister deserves a lot of the credit."

Spare me the dogmatic rhetoric. "Every Member of Parliament did our part to protect our citizens and our way of life. Thankfully, the covid-19 crisis is behind us. The past is prologue for what is to come." Poirier leaned forward, elbows on his knees. Fingers laced. "The prime minister seems very determined to take all guns away from Canadians not in military or law enforcement uniforms."

"Well, at least this time the amendment is following the proper parliamentary process."

"That remains to be seen. I'm not convinced Reid will let it die If Parliament and the people we serve don't agree with him. Another order-in-council from cabinet, perhaps?"

"I don't think that's very likely."

"Anything is possible. The projected cost of the buyback fluctuates daily. I think it's a low ball estimate that our pandemic bludgeoned and bled national budget cannot absorb." Poirier studied Lockwood's obvious slump and fidgeting movements. I've jabbed his pain point. On to point two. "Then there's the porous border with the gun-worshipping United States. Once all weapons are illegal in Canada, how do we keep them out of the hands of illegal owners?"

Lockwood's spine stiffened. His knuckles rapped the table. "That's exactly the argument I tried to bring up with the Director of Parliamentary Protective Service."

Poirier's eyebrows raised and arched over the black rims of his glasses. "Oh? What did the chief superintendent have to say?"

"He brushed me off. Said he couldn't comment."

"In politics, no comment speaks volumes."

"The PPS director isn't a politician."

"No. But he's married to the prime minister's gatekeeper. What Reid knows, she knows." Poirier's magnified stare sized up his prey. "I want to know if I can count on you, Vincent. When the committee convenes to consider the second reading of this amendment, will you ask the questions and discuss your concerns? Or will you stay silent and blindly vote with your party and prime minister?"

Lockwood coughed into the hand at his mouth and cleared his throat. "I've always voiced my concerns and spoken up for my constituents."

"So we agree. The amendment should not pass in its present form."

"Look, I won't just kill the bill without discussing the alternatives. I firmly believe the amendment should pass out of committee for second reading. This must be on the agenda, and tabled for third reading, if that's how Parliament votes. The final decision isn't up to us or the committee. Every MP has a voice. Every MP votes."

How incredibly short-sighted and sanctimonious you are. How typically and pathetically Liberal. Poirier applied direct pressure to stop the debate and force a simple response. "Do we agree the amendment should not pass out of committee as entered on first reading. Yes or no."

Lockwood momentarily held his breath and released an answer. "Yes. On that we agree."

"That's all I needed to know." Poirier stood. "Enjoy what's left of your holiday break." He walked Lockwood to his office door and turned back to his assistant. "You may go as well, Douglas. Have those notes ready for me by nine tomorrow morning." He closed the door behind them. And sneered.

"Fools." Poirier sat at his desk, lifted the receiver on the landline phone, and called the lone New Democrat Party MP on his public safety committee. "Hello, Sydney. How was your holiday? So your time away has been productive? Good to hear. I'd like to meet and discuss committee strategy on the Liberals handgun ban amendment. No, before the next session. Just the two of us. My office? At your convenience, of course. Tomorrow at three? Excellent." Poirier made a similar call to a Bloc Quebecois MP he was certain could be swayed. Tasks completed to his satisfaction, he slipped into his topcoat and picked up the cell phone. "Hello, my darling. Have you had dinner yet? No? Is the nanny still there? Good. Ask her to stay the evening. I feel like celebrating."

Chapter 7

Jerilynn

The ping signal of an incoming text message interrupted a pointless conversation that I'd been waiting for an excuse to close.

"Je comprends votre inquiétude." I understand your concern. *"Oui, bien sûr, je vous le ferai savoir."* Yes, of course I will let you know. *"Merci. Au revoir."*

Hi Jerilynn. It's Margot, read the text. I just got in. Are you free to meet for coffee?

I checked my schedule. Two hours with no commitments.

Sure, I texted back. Our usual place?

I'll see you there in ten minutes.

Deceptive sunlight warmed the spirit but did nothing to chase away the actual chill. I crossed my arms and hugged my closed coat tight against me along the short distance walk from Parliament Hill to the cozy spot Margot and I had claimed as ours. Off the beaten path and out of the way of political snoops with loose lips. Or so we thought.

Margot waved at me through the glass store front from the window table she'd scored. Warmed air, digitally recorded smooth jazz and the delicious smell of ground coffee, herbal tea and fresh baked muffins both stimulated and soothed me on the inside.

"Happy New Year." We gave each other a quick hug and ordered lattes. "How was your holiday break?" Margot asked.

"Good, but short." I told her about our just-the-two-of-us Christmas and the New Year's Eve party at Rideau Cottage.

"So you didn't go back to Nova Scotia to visit your families?"

"No. It seems whenever we try one of us gets called back early. We're thinking about making the trip to Liverpool sometime this summer before the fall election campaign starts. How about you?"

"Well, I don't have family in Lethbridge. So I volunteered at the food bank, helped out at church, got together with friends and fellow hospital retirees." She fingered the silk scarf around her neck with nails stylishly painted the same coral color. I couldn't recall ever seeing Margot without her signature fashion statement accessory. "They gave me a bouquet of scarves for my birthday so I'd be set for the upcoming session of Parliament."

"Well, happy birthday," I said and touched my paper cup with hers. "When was it and I won't ask how many years."

"Two days after Christmas and I don't mind revealing my age. I'm fifty-five and I wear it well." She sighed and stuck a stir stick in her latte. "It's hard to believe Ben has been gone almost six years now. He proposed to me on Christmas Eve twenty-eight years ago."

"The holidays have to be tough for you to get through. It sure would be for me. Alec and I just celebrated our seventh anniversary on New Year's Eve. I can't imagine …"

"Then don't go there. Enjoy every day you have together now. What's to come will happen in its time."

I sat back in the simple wooden chair that didn't quite match the one Margot was in and smiled at the opposition party MP. "You remind me of my mother. You always know exactly what to say."

She smiled back. "If I could have had a daughter, I would have wanted her to be like you. I mean, how many women can type on a laptop while holding a cup of coffee and not spill a drop on her suit?"

I scrunched my nose as if that might help me remember. "What? Oh, you mean the day we sort of stumbled across each other in the West Block north wing?"

"Yes, indeed. Strangers with no idea who the other was." Margot covered her chin with her palm. "I'm glad that hasn't kept us from chats over coffee." Movement past the window got her attention. "Or maybe I spoke too soon."

The prime minister rapped his knuckles on the coffee shop's store front window without breaking stride. The look he shot me through the glass sent a shiver from my neck to my heels and a clear message. "*I'm not pleased and your explanation had better be good.*"

"Duty calls." I slid my arms into my coat and slung my purse over my shoulder.

"You better have a good answer," Margot said.

I hurried toward and through the door. Protection detail officers trotted to keep up with the long, brisk strides of my four inches over six foot tall boss. I ran on much shorter legs to catch up.

"Why did you come looking for me?" I puffed, short of breath, and vowed to start using the treadmill in our basement as intended rather than as a clothesline for drying towels. "You could have called."

"You could have maintained the proper protocol."

"Oh, so now I need permission to leave Parliament Hill?"

The muscles in his jaw tightened. The abrupt stop in his determined forward advance scrambled the detail. I tripped and hopped over a crack in the sidewalk. *Uh, oh, Jerilynn,* I thought. *This time you've really poked the bear.*

"We will save this discussion for my office," he said in low tone clipped delivery.

We walked the rest of the way in silence.

I lagged behind on the spiral stairway to his office. My boss took the steps two at a time, opened his office door and tossed his coat on a chair. He sat at his desk, elbows bent and anchored on the chair's arms, fingertips together and spread apart. I closed the door, shimmied out of my coat and dropped into my usual spot. Few have seen my boss battle the lightning bolts of anger he once told me his father warned him that he must learn to control. I stayed silent as he struggled to calm the storm within.

"You are skating on precariously thin ice."

"I did nothing wrong. Margot and I know what we can and cannot discuss."

As soon as I said it, I knew it was the wrong answer. He hadn't looked at me since the walk-with-me-right-now glance through the coffee shop window. The smoldering storm had darkened his eyes to a shade of dangerously pissed off. I withered in my seat. "Oh, do you? Well, now, that's reassuring. I'm certain the Conservative Party whip will be pleased to know the Honourable Margot Isley from the Alberta riding of Lethbridge isn't sharing caucus business with the Liberal Party prime minister's chief of staff. Do you not understand the political implications?"

"Are you saying you don't trust me?"

"Of course not! If I didn't trust you, you wouldn't be in my office! This is not a question of trust. It is a matter of indiscretion and impropriety that I cannot ignore, excuse or defend."

Back off. You know he's right. "I'm sorry. I should and I do know better. Margot and I shouldn't have continued these casual chats. We had a very innocent first meeting a week or so after the last election when neither of us knew the role and title of the other. I guess we just filled each other's void. This is her first term, she's a widow and she's a long way from home. She spent most of her life as a doctor taking care of people but couldn't save her husband. You and I both know this life we've chosen doesn't leave a lot of time for family or friends. I guess Margot substituted a bit of both for me."

He took a deep breath and leaned back in his chair. Step two in his anger management regimen. "Jerilynn, I totally understand. But the reality of life in politics is that we must follow the rules or our credibility and integrity is lost. Without that, we cannot expect to be respected. If I condone a double standard in my office or my government I am not fit to lead." He swiveled in his chair and stared into a place where no one else could go. We sat in the quiet opposite the Centre Block government fortress under renovation for a return to its original glory. "Can I ask you a personal question?"

"Of course."

"Did you ever wish you'd made a different career choice?"

What's this about? "No. Every decision and move I made put me closer to exactly where I wanted to be. Right here."

When he looked at me, the sadness and longing that suddenly surrounded him, like heavy clouds on a day full of rain, knotted my chest. I wanted to console him, shed a tear for him. But for the life of me I couldn't figure out why.

"I envy you."

I waited for more but he offered nothing.

A return to duty broke the spell. "Let's get to work on the C-71 amendment second reading."

"Yes, Prime Minister."

Chapter 8

The Threat

An abrupt drop in temperature transformed sheets of cold rain into fat flakes of wet snow. The weather obscured the Pacific Ocean view on the other side of the high and wide windows.

Myrna Rosen shuttled a tray of hot coffee in two-tone brown cups and a plate stacked with treats from her kitchen to the table in the open dining area. Eight years had passed since she and her partner had claimed and rebuilt the compact four room home in the wilds midway between the northern and southern tips of Vancouver Island. They took pride in their independence and fiercely defended their living-off-the-grid choice. Long gun hunting and their garden fed them. Hand guns kept four and two-legged predators off their property.

Myrna settled her wide hips and buttocks on the bench next to her partner. Diabetes prohibited her from eating the rich chocolate Nanaimo bars loaded with fudge layered on a honey coated graham cracker crust. The disease had also taken away the scoop of sugar she usually stirred into her coffee. Myrna drank it black now. She tasted from memory every bite and sweet sip taken by her thinner healthier partner and envied the natural ash blonde braid down her back. Myrna missed being blonde. She didn't much care for her own dusty silver.

"The Ottawa connection came through." The younger woman spoke directly to the big man seated on the bench across the table from her. "Two hundred fifty thousand dollars has been wired into the account. He's promised to double that in three days."

He licked chocolate and crumbs from his fingers and lips. "The account is in Myrna's name?"

"Yes. For now. We'll move it to another account when the next wire transfer comes in."

"I say we spend it." The second man stopped pacing the room and reached for a cup of coffee. A fresh tattoo on his wrist flamed red around black numbers. His network member code. "Buy the guns. Start blowing things up. Let that puny piece of shit PM know we mean business."

"We agreed to wait. Going in hot would tip our hand, Troy."

I thought we'd left Lethbridge behind us, Sylvie, thought Myrna. *Why is your psychotic cousin Troy sitting at our table?*

Deep lines scrawled white in contrast to his red-faced flush of spontaneous anger. "We also agreed no names, Sylvia!"

"Both of you stand down!" The big man slapped his fleshy palms on the table. Coffee spilled. Treats toppled.

Myrna jumped.

"The attacks must appear random. Bar room brawls in the territories and small towns. Major damage in locations specifically tied to the prime minister and his family. We'll move west to east. First Victoria. Then Saskatoon. Toronto. Gatineau right before we hit Ottawa. No guns until and only at Parliament Hill."

"What's the point to that strategy?" Troy demanded.

"Distraction from the target with just enough clues to make the game interesting." The big man bit into a second layered bar and grinned. "God, how I'll enjoy watching those backwater detachment losers pick up bricks tossed through windows and chase their tails to dead ends. They kicked me out of the academy. I wasn't good enough for the RCMP. Alec Martin is their golden boy, probably on his way up to commissioner. Well, I'm going to fuck with his head. He'll follow the bread crumbs I drop. He's probably the only one in the ranks with enough balls and brains to figure it out." He licked crumbles of crust from cracked lips and sucked chocolate off the tips of his thick fingers. "By the time Smart Alec puts it together, I'll be in position. And the person he's paid big bucks to take a bullet for will be dead. A casualty of civil war."

Myrna's attempt to stifle a loud gasp failed. Dirty cups collected on the tray in her hands quivered. The tea kettle on the wood-fired kitchen stove tweeted to shrill. Myrna mixed hot water with the cold she'd pumped from the well into the single-well sink. She busied herself with cleanup until the front door closed. A cotton hand towel dried the tears on her cheeks. She shivered under her partner's arm around her waist.

"Are they gone?" Myrna asked.

"Yes." Sylvia leaned her head on her partner's shoulder. "What's wrong, Big Sis?" Her term of endearment for the woman she loved usually cleared the air ahead of the storm.

"How can you ask me that?" Myrna tossed the hand towel on the wooden drain board. She stepped away and turned to confront the friend she'd nursed back to physical and emotional health after her abusive ex broke her cheekbone with his fist. The police failed to prove beyond reasonable doubt that Troy had torched the truck with the body of his cousin's former lover inside. "When did you hook up with that animal again?"

Sylvia shrugged and tugged at her braid. "Troy is in the network of concerned citizens who will stop that dictator Reid from taking away our guns. So am I. I told you about that."

"You didn't tell me he was involved or that this network is planning a murder!"

"James was just bragging, talking tough."

"So what are the guns he talked tough about going to be used for?"

"The network protestors that already have legal licenses will carry them as props on the day Parliament debates and votes on the handgun amendment. The guns won't be loaded. The network will get permits from the city of Ottawa. It's all legit."

"I don't know, Sylvie. I don't like this. We already know what Troy is capable of. And that guy James scares me. He's got an axe to grind with the RCMP and whoever Alec Martin is that has nothing to do with keeping our guns."

"C'mere." Sylvia hugged Myrna and hummed a tune she knew would soothe her. "Haven't we always walked away when the trouble passes? This too shall pass, Big Sis. We'll survive and rise above it."

Myrna went through the usual routine motions that night. She lay next to Sylvia and listened for the regular breaths of sleep. Slow and patient movements lifted the heavy quilt and Myrna's weight from the mattress. She padded barefoot to the junk drawer in the kitchen and inched it slowly forward. Groping fingers found the address book. She turned back the laminated cover over stenciled images of pink flowers and blue birds and flipped through the pages. Myrna had erased or blacked out all the Lethbridge contacts. Except one. The name and phone number of the ER doctor who had helped Sylvia, referred her for counseling, and befriended them both.

Margot is an MP now. I've got to tell her. Warn her. She'll know what to do.

The call went to voice mail. Myrna left a message. "Margot. It's Myrna. Please call me back as soon as you can. I don't know who Alec Martin is. But he needs to hear what I know." She hid the address book under a stained tea towel and slid the drawer closed.

Chapter 9

Victoria, British Columbia

The man and woman outfitted in costumes considered so vile that they'd scoped out a nearby dumpster for rapid disposal stood across the street from a place they'd both rather torch than enter.

Troy sneered at patrons dressed in skin-tight jeans and flamboyant colored garments similar to what hugged and tugged at his and her well-proportioned bodies. "I hate this." He spit on the sidewalk to emphasize his disgust. "I'd sooner eat my 45 Colt than rub elbows with a bar full of queers."

"Keep your mind on what we're here to do." The cell phone Sylvia had tucked in the small white satin handbag looped around her wrist pinged and vibrated. "Let's go."

They stepped off the curb and avoided cars stopped in traffic and parked in front of the bar. The burly bouncer with tips of closely-cropped hair dyed lime green earned the two-hundred dollar tip they'd paid him. He let them in, muscled through the crowd waiting for drinks and tables, and led them to the reserved table next to the rear door marked exit.

The carnage began with the 'in place' signal sent from her cell phone to two more network comrades nearby and outside. The first softball-sized rock thrown from the street through the front window shattered a full pitcher of beer in the center of a table of friends celebrating an accepted proposal of marriage.

Thrown bottles shattered the establishment's custom-made name and logo mirror behind the bar. Stools doubled as battering rams. The rotten egg odor of accelerant used to set fires in cars parked behind the building fouled the air to the brink of non-breathable.

Fifteen minutes were all they needed to ruin a Saturday night out near the heart of an older affluent neighborhood in British Columbia's capital city. The trendy Victoria business that had closed, reopened and recovered from the pandemic sustained major damage. Thirty-two people who had come out to enjoy the mild January thaw evening were transported to hospital for treatment of injuries ranging from cuts that required stitches to overnight admissions for concussions and fractured bones.

At Troy's signal, members of the network ran from the chaos they'd created and down a side street to a parked car concealed by privet hedge. Doors opened and closed. Headlight beams spot lit and shadowed the two-story white house with the wrap-around porch across the street owned by Celine Reid and her sons Evan and Jonathan.

They'd escaped the first hit unharmed, unseen and unidentified. All had gone according to plan.

Chapter 10

Willie

Routine rounds at the mid-point of his shift ended as always in the break room. Willie lifted a nearly empty glass carafe from the coffee maker, sniffed at the semi-scorched contents and went about the business of making a fresh pot.

Henry Schaughnessy, Willie's Parliament Hill security guard companion every Monday into Tuesday, Tuesday into Wednesday and Thursday night until early Friday morning, shuffled a deck of playing cards and laid out a game of solitaire.

"You could play that on your smartphone if you had one," Willie said.

"That would break two time honoured traditions," Henry responded. "Cards were made for playing and phones aren't meant to be smart."

Willie set his coffee-stained cup with the Maple Leafs logo and the chipped lip on the table and sat across from Henry. He stretched his arms overhead and tried to stifle a yawn.

"Not sleeping?" Henry asked.

"Not as much as I'd like to."

"It's all in the timing. After hunkering down in foxholes, I knew I could sleep anywhere and make it count whenever I got the chance."

Willie grunted. "Sometimes I feel like I'm living in a war zone."

Henry glanced up from his game. "Still rough at home?"

"Yeah, and getting worse with this ban the handgun bill. The old man has taken to ranting about how Prince Privileged the oppressor is taking away our guns. I don't know why he's so upset about it."

"Does he own a handgun?"

"No. We've never had guns in the house. He doesn't hunt and he's not a veteran like you. As far as I know, he's never even held a gun, much less fired one."

"Wasn't he a Tory MP?"

"Yeah, for one term."

"Been a card-carrying Conservative Party member all his life, I'll bet."

"You got that right."

"Well, then there you have it. Wouldn't make any difference what the issue is. If a Liberal Party PM wants it, the Tories are against it."

"Even if most of the people are for it?"

"That's the way it works in Ottawa. Politics overrules democracy unless the rules favor the politicians."

"What about you? You've been in the military. Didn't you say you took this part time job after you retired from the Ottawa police department?

"That's right."

"So what's your stand on making handguns illegal?"

Henry scooped up and re-shuffled the cards. "There's nothing wrong with owning a handgun or a firearm of any kind as long as you have a valid license, lock it up properly at home, and have an authorization to transport it to a range or gun show. Or get an authorization to carry like I have."

"How did you get an authorization to carry?"

"Security guard clearance."

"But we don't carry guns."

Henry winked at Willie. "Veteran and former cop. And I know how to use a gun. Too many people with guns don't. That's the biggest problem, aside from the guns that are stolen from legal owners or smuggled in from outside Canada."

"Dad keeps ranting about how it's not up to the government to tell people they can't defend themselves."

"That's bullshit. Those folks need to get off their fat asses and take karate lessons. At least then they won't shoot themselves or somebody else by accident. Or worse yet get in the way of a cop trying to do his or her job."

"Will you teach me how to shoot a gun?" Willie asked.

Henry's casual expression changed to puzzled concern. "Why do you want to learn?"

Willie pressed fingers into his temples for precious seconds of relief from the constant throb in his head. He sat back in the chair and fought to relax shoulders hunched up around his ringing ears. "I tried karate and quit. Dad said I lacked discipline. What I lack is coordination."

Henry's clucking chuckle returned the mood of the conversation to casual. "Sure. I'll take you out to the range. Just let me know when." He looked down at the cards and frowned. "This was a bad hand. I'm going out for a smoke."

"How can you do that without tripping an alarm?"

Henry picked up a playing card from the table. "Trick of the trade made easier with the renovations going on in Centre Block. In and out and no one is the wiser. C'mon. I'll show you."

The route to Henry's smoke break escape portal took Willie down corridors he didn't know were there. Evident remnants of areas under construction littered the path that led to the partially hidden door. He held up the playing card. "This gets it open and this," he nudged a cement block with the side of his shoe, "keeps it open until I'm ready to come back in. Observe." He slid the playing card between the door frame and the lock and waited for the red locking sensor light to turn green. "Push the door, shove the block and step on through."

The cold rush of air ruffled Willie's hair. He rubbed his palms over the goosebumps under his shirt. Willie watched Henry fold and secure the playing card in the sliver of metal layers that held the door frame together. "Is it really that easy?" Willie asked.

"Easy as using a credit card on a locked door that doesn't need a key." Henry lit up, took several deep draws on the cigarette, dropped the butt on the ground, stepped on and snubbed it out. He bent over to pick it up and stuffed it in his shirt pocket. "Leave no evidence."

"Would this work to get in the building? The playing card trick, I mean."

"I don't see why not. It's the same lock. You'd just need to close the door quickly before the red light comes back on."

They parted duty paths on the stroll back to the break room. Willie finished his coffee and got ready for another routine walk through the West Block.

Chapter 11

February ~ Alec

The sweet and sour of instant communication through modern technology hit my desk simultaneously a half hour before quitting time.

I feel like chicken tonight read the text from the beautiful and brilliant love of my life.

You're in luck I texted back. Roast bird with garlic mashed potatoes and a side of honey-glazed carrots and snap peas are on the menu.

I'll pick up dessert she answered.

The email alert chimed before I could text back my 'something with whipped cream' request to smooth on her breasts and other luscious parts.

From: Commanding Officer K Division RCMP Headquarters Edmonton

To: Chief Superintendent Alec Martin Director of Parliamentary Protective Service

Subject: Safety and security threat

While the overall content of the message didn't surprise me, the uncertainty of the depth and potential reach of the network to deliver the threat did. Groups protesting stricter gun control laws identified through social media and peaceful gatherings marred by violent incidents were nothing new. But the communiqué out of Alberta's provincial capital warned of links posted covertly under code numbers with no names attached. The incident counts began to pop a week after a gay bar in Victoria was trashed and patrons injured by unknown assailants. This attack had to be more than a random hate crime. K Division described a pattern of hits on targets from the west coast into Alberta heading east toward Saskatchewan. The strategy behind the action implied a threat to parliamentarians as the handgun ban amendment passed from committee to the House of Commons.

I acknowledged receipt of the email, requested updates as available and headed home to roast chicken. The cell phone in my pocket buzzed with the click of my closed office door. Unknown caller flashed on the screen. *This has to be a wrong number. Incoming calls on my cell always display contact names, locations or call back numbers.* Those that don't aren't answered. I let it go to voice mail. No message. The phone rang again seconds later. Again, the unknown caller left no message. I answered the third call on the second ring. "Who is this?"

"Victoria was a warm up. Saskatoon is next." The caller hung up. Call back didn't work. The burner phone used was most likely trashed.

How the hell did that dickhead get this cell number? My fists and jaw clenched. *Why Victoria and Saskatoon? What's the connection?* I went back into my office and fired up the computer.

From: Chief Superintendent Alec Martin Director of Parliamentary Protective Service

To: Commanding Officer F Division RCMP Headquarters Saskatchewan

CC: Christine Burke, RCMP Commissioner; Saskatoon detachment

Subject: Safety and security threat Saskatoon

Source and intended target unknown. Timeline uncertain. Anonymous caller referenced Victoria incident. Prepare for possible attack on similar business and/or public location in Saskatoon.

Chapter 12

Jerilynn

Pastry and gelato from 'Little Italy' shops enticed until I thought about the treadmill vow made while I trotted beside my boss, out of breath and panting like a dog on a hot summer day. I stopped at the grocery and purchased expensive out-of-season strawberries instead.

Chef Alec was at work in the kitchen shoving an onion in the cavity of a whole chicken. A pot half-filled with water waited on the stove for the white chunks of peeled potatoes piled on the cutting board. I took the strawberries from the reusable cloth bag and set the recyclable container on the shades of grey flecked granite island centered in our kitchen and used to prep, serve, sit and eat most of our meals.

"Hey, handsome." A quick peck on the lips was never enough for either of us.

"Give me a minute, gorgeous." He reached for a stick of butter wrapped in paper.

"Can we go a little lighter on the calories?" I asked.

"A chicken without butter is like a day without sex. No flavor and nothing to look forward to."

He moved away from my rib poke. "OK, we'll compromise." He cut the stick in half with a knife and dotted the skin with globs of yellow fat. "Open the oven door, will you m'lady?"

"Of course, kind sir."

The chicken went in. His hands, wiped clean and dried on a dish towel, went around my waist. "Now for the main course." His kiss, soft at first, deepened with the flick of his tongue on and between my lips. He groaned when I did the same. "What's for dessert?" His tongue trailed the skin exposed with each unbutton of the buttons on my blouse.

"Strawberries."

"I don't suppose we have any whipped cream."

The ring tone of the cell phone still in my jacket pocket interrupted our pre-dinner foreplay. "Hold that thought," I said and checked the caller ID.

Hi, Margot. Listen, .."

"It's OK," she said. "I already got reprimanded by my party's whip."

"I'm sorry."

"Apology not necessary. I'm way out of line calling you. I may even be told to take a one way trip back to Lethbridge. If you have to hang up on me, do it now."

I quickly dismissed the political need to follow protocol. "I'm listening."

"There are a lot of people in my riding who aren't happy about the prime minister's anti-gun bill."

"Tell me something I don't know."

"I'd dismissed the complaints as the usual noise. Then I got a phone call from a friend who was obviously frightened by what she'd heard at a meeting in B.C. and reached out to me for help. She didn't go into a lot of detail. She's not directly involved. She said they're organizing in small groups and the strategy is covert. All word of mouth recruitment. No printed propaganda or even social media. No public protests until the final day of debate and vote on the handgun amendment in the House of Commons. She said the money to buy guns is coming from a source in Ottawa. The only name mentioned was your husband's along with an unspecified death threat. I have no idea what they are planning. But it can't be good. I gotta go. Take care."

I leaned against the island and stared at the phone in my hand.

"Should I hold off on dinner?"

"What, love?"

"Do you have to go?"

"No." My mind raced to cloudy conclusions that frightened me for undefined reasons.

"What is it, honey?"

"I think you need to increase security around my boss."

"Why?"

I sensed he already knew and was waiting for me to tell him. "With this gun bill debate coming up, I just think it's a good idea."

"With you, nothing is that straight forward. So are you gonna tell me who was on the phone?"

"I really shouldn't."

He frowned and turned away from me. "Fine." He plopped the potatoes into the pot of water and lit the burner underneath.

I put the cell phone back in my jacket pocket and crossed my arms over my chest. "But it seems I have to." I told him about meeting up with Margot and the prime minister's reprimand. "I still think he overreacted. Who I have coffee with is personal, not political."

"Honey, in Ottawa everything is political, from who you're seen with, where you have coffee, or what brand of soup you buy in what store."

"That's a bit of an exaggeration."

"Not by much. So I'm guessing that was the MP on the phone that your boss told you in no uncertain terms was off limits."

"It was."

"Now that I've guessed who called, are you going to tell me what was so important that she risked her Conservative Party neck?"

I told him our conversation nearly word-for-word as I could remember. "Now what do you have to tell me?"

"What makes you think I have anything to spill?"

"Your reaction when I said the prime minister needs more protection."

My husband opened the refrigerator and grabbed packages of fresh carrots and peas from the slide out crisper. "I got a high level alert message from the RCMP Divisional Headquarters in Edmonton today that basically confirms what your MP friend just told you."

"Wow."

"You can say that again. But please don't." He talked as he mixed and poured honey glaze over the vegetables. "Any ideas on who the Ottawa bagman might be?"

"Bagman?"

"The link between who has the money and what needs it."

"I wish I did. But I'm damn sure going to find out."

Honey glaze dripped from the spoon he pointed at me. "No, you won't. You'll stay out of it."

"Why?"

"Because that's my job. Guns, money, politics and the lunatic fringe are a dangerous combination."

"But I have daily access to the probable targets and possible suspects."

"That's exactly why you'll keep your distance and not ask questions." He turned down the gas flame under the boiling pot of potatoes. And turned to me. "Has anyone asked you for my cell phone number?"

"No, and I wouldn't give it out if I were asked."

"I didn't think so."

"Then why did you ask?"

"Somebody has it who shouldn't."

"Any ideas on who?"

"Not a clue. But I will find out who it is and how he got it."

Our lovemaking that night was as subdued as the conversation over dinner. We held each other in the quiet and calm without knowing how soon or even how it would end.

"You can't tell anyone that Margot called or what she said. That would be a serious breach of our marital contract and bedroom confidentiality."

"So how do I explain the order of increased security around the PM?"

"You'll think of something."

"I suppose I can use the volatility of the gun bill as an excuse to request extra detail. But it's going to be up to you to come up with a white lie when he notices and asks and you know he will."

"I'll think of something."

He hugged me close in the warmth and strength of him and kissed my forehead. "I have no doubt of that."

Chapter 13

Willie

Sweat soaked the bed sheets Willie woke up between. The pillow over his head hadn't quite drowned out the cacophony of his father's latest rant of rage aimed at the Liberal Party prime minister. Darkness outside his bedroom window where even street light beams wouldn't reach meant he'd probably slept through dinner. He kicked off the sheets, stripped off damp boxers and t-shirt and grabbed a robe from the hook on the back of his bedroom door. A long shower would clean his outer skin. But Willie knew nothing could refresh his weary to-the-bone body and demoralized soul.

Freshly scrubbed and dried, Willie covered what he had to with clean underwear and the robe and stepped into slippers. He took a deep breath to settle his nerves and descended the stairs.

"So good of you to join us." His father sat at the kitchen table. Two fingers of scotch swirled in the glass he held by the rim and rotated in a clockwise circular motion with his wrist. "Please." He kicked the chair across from his with his foot. "Have a seat." William Senior brought the glass to his lips, tipped his head back and swallowed. He raised the empty glass above his receding hairline. "Rose," he ordered his wife. "Pour me another and get our son a bowl of food."

"It's OK, Mom," Willie said. "I'll get my own."

"I told you to sit down!" His father shouted and kicked the chair again.

Willie could tell from the heavy tongue slur that his dad had been drinking before, during and since dinner. His mother silently shuffled between cupboards and stove. Willie stared down at the bowl of beef vegetable soup she'd set in front of him. Although his stomach growled, the steam and smell from the homemade mixture of lean meat, potatoes, carrots, celery, broth and dumplings nauseated him. He dipped the spoon his mother had handed him into the soup and tried not to notice the tremble in her aged hands as she poured two more fingers of scotch into his father's glass.

"Leave it," he told her. The slumped shoulders beneath her house-coat bowed a bit more. She set the half-empty bottle in front of him and escaped to her corner in the sun room where music and news on the radio kept her company.

"So, William. How's life in the fast lane on Parliament Hill?"

Willie stirred the soup. "Pretty quiet at night."

"It's a bit livelier during the day. But you wouldn't know that. Not like I did." Senior gulped the scotch and poured another. "First that fancy pants bastard prime minister legalized wacky weed, which helped you out by the way. Wiped your possession record clean. I guess you wouldn't have needed your old man's MP pull to get you that cushy full time job taking naps in between walks around the hallowed halls."

"I don't take naps."

"And I'm not an MP anymore." Senior glowered over the glass under his nose. "Now Prince Privileged wants to take personal property from legally licensed gun owners. It wasn't enough to come up with an arbitrary list of fifteen hundred banned firearms. Oh, no! Let's stick the taxpayers with the bill to buyback those guns at a loss to the owners THEN ban handguns and run up the tax tab even more!" He slammed down two more shots and pointed the middle finger of the hand around the glass at Willie. "Did I ever tell you I knew Tony Reid?"

Willie slurped a spoonful of broth. "Many times."

"Well, he's spinning in his grave. Evan Reid may be his son, but he's no Tony Reid. That prime minister had power and he knew how to wield it. And he sure as hell wouldn't have used it to make pot legal and guns illegal. This imitation has no plan of action to back up his flowery speeches and folds under pressure when the going gets tough. From my first thought in the morning to the last before I fall sleep, I still cannot understand how Canadians could be so fooled. Not once but TWICE!" Senior slammed the glass on the table with a force that cracked the glass. "What a disappointment my life has been!"

So the tirade begins, Willie thought. The groan stuck in his throat.

"I went to law school in Ottawa with the intent and goal of making my mark in Conservative Party politics. I envisioned leaving a legacy of low taxation, a balanced budget, and opportunity for every Canadian willing to work hard to provide for themselves and their families and grow our economy to sustain that prosperity for future generations. I finally reached my goal as a Member of Parliament after years in Ontario provincial politics only to have that dream taken from me by the Liberal Party and that backbench piss ant with the infamous last name! I walk past Parliament Hill every morning and night on my way to and from another boring as shit day of contract law. I come home to a mousy woman who birthed a tin soldier guard without a gun and a glorified barber."

"Annabel is a licensed cosmetologist and massage therapist."

"She's a fucking barber who got knocked up at nineteen by some guy and didn't bother to ask him his name. I keep a roof over her head, pay for my granddaughter to go to the best private school in Ottawa and do I get any thanks for my trouble? Not from Fiona! She's a smart mouthed, lazy teenager who taunts and insults me! You know what she said to me at dinner tonight? DO YOU, WILLIAM?" he shouted.

"How could I, huh? As you pointed out, I wasn't at dinner. I was trying to sleep."

Senior rose from his chair and leaned over the table. "She said I lost both elections because I'm an old and ugly relic and called Prince Privileged HOT!" His face was as red as the actual definition and description of the last word he'd shouted at Willie. "What the FUCK does THAT mean?"

"It means she thinks he's good-looking." Willie went to the sink, dumped the soup he couldn't eat down the garbage disposal, and rinsed out the bowl.

"Since when did good-looking qualify a man to be prime minister!"

"I'm going out." Willie climbed the stairs and dressed in his work uniform. The door at the end of the hall slammed. The television in his parents' bedroom blared distorted dialogue. Willie swallowed a scream. He grabbed the faded Maple Leaf jacket and winced with the jabs of pain at the base of his skull caused by each jarring step down the stairs. The ambient light in the kitchen cast shadowed ghostly shapes of pans hanging from hooks on the pot rack over the sink. He heard his mother humming along to a song on the radio.

If I left for good, would you go with me, Mom? Willie glanced at the family portrait she'd hung on the wall fifteen years ago. Framed faces without smiles under dust-coated glass. *If we were gone would he notice?* Willie left the house three hours before night shift check in. He spent the time alone at Timmy's drinking coffee and playing Call of Duty on his smartphone.

Chapter 14

Saskatoon, Saskatchewan

The owner of the bar and grill hummed a tune from her childhood, a song her grandmother had sung every Sunday morning in the Hope Fellowship Church choir. Business had nearly doubled since Olivia's restaurant had been licensed to serve liquor six months ago. The city hall struggle with parents and teachers concerned about the proximity of a bar to a kindergarten through grade eight public school had been two years long. But the profit from increased patronage had been worth it. Most of the thirty-six chairs at nine four-top tables and four stools at the counter were occupied on weekend nights and this Saturday was no exception. Olivia served draft and bottled beers to customers at the counter and pulled the cork on a fourth bottle of chardonnay.

A disagreement between two men wearing orange and yellow road work safety vests who had seated themselves at the table near the rear exit escalated to a shouting match. Olivia thought about asking them to take their argument about the federal handgun ban elsewhere when another customer shouted "Fire!" and pointed toward the window with a rear view of the parking lot. Flames leapt from the interior of the sedan and licked at the roof through the broken driver's side window. She called 9-1-1 just as a thrown brick splintered a gaping hole in the front door.

The men in safety vests stood and hurled their bottles at the walls. Beer streamed down the chintz plum blossom wallpaper that Olivia had meticulously trimmed and smoothed over stained brown paneling. Customers screamed and huddled under tables. Plastic tubs filled with unwashed glasses, utensils and dishes slid from overturned tray jacks to the green and white square floor tiles. Wait staff ran for cover behind the kitchen's swinging door.

"Stop! Please stop!" She begged the men who were destroying what she'd invested her life savings and dreams in. She squatted for cover under the counter. Long arms swept bottles of wine and spirits from shelves behind the bar. Ribbons of red and gold flowed over shards of fractured glass like a sudden stream over pebbles, a dry creek bed fed by a flash flood.

"Send the bill to the prime minister," she heard one of them say. The others laughed.

Sirens wailed on the city street. Olivia sobbed into a bar rag.

Chapter 15

Alec

Questions asked the day after the specifics of my vague communiqué were made violently evident and real had no answers and led nowhere. Suspect descriptions from victims and eyewitnesses to the mounting number of apparently unprovoked attacks in all four western provinces didn't match up. Property damage and minor injuries had been reported at the scene of every assault inflicted in small town public places. Major damage, more serious injuries and torched cars only in Victoria and Saskatoon set these particular incidents apart.

"I hate it when things don't make sense." Colin Landry, my operations officer, stared at the paper pile of notated frustration.

"I hate waiting." I nudged the cell phone staring face up at me from the table, as if my thumb could trigger a text or call. "I know the chances of a trace are less than zero. But I'd still like to have that chance."

"Even another lead on the next target is better than nothing." Colin took off the glasses he wore out of eyestrain relief need toward the end of long days. He blinked at the retreating stream of sunlight through windows in my office where we'd spent most of this particular long day. "Alberta seems to be ground zero. Bar brawls in Red Deer, Lethbridge, Medicine Hat, Lacombe and Leduc. Manitoba hasn't been spared. Steinbach and Selkirk police have had their hands full. But where's the pattern? Victoria has been the only provincial capital hit. And hit hard like the place in Saskatoon. But one was a gay bar the other a diner with a liquor license. It doesn't make sense."

"They're heading east. The closer they get to our back yard, the more we'll be authorized to do and the deeper the PPS can dig." My cell phone buzzed. J-lynn's name popped up on the display. "What's up, love?"

"My car is dead. The remote start didn't and the door won't unlock."

"Are you on The Hill?"

"Yes. I'm trying to punch through ice in the lock with my key. There! Got it. Now the challenge is turning the key in the lock."

"Hang on, honey. I'll be right there." I ended the call and grabbed my coat. "J-lynn's car won't start."

"Can I help?"

"It probably just needs a jump." My phone chimed an incoming text message alert. "Maybe she's already got help." My wife was in the photo attached to the text message. But the image of her getting in her car wasn't taken in the nearby parking lot. *What the fuck!* "That's our townhouse!"

Colin leaned over my shoulder and read the message. "Seven ten."

"That's when she leaves for work." J-lynn walked toward the West Block in the next photo. The text read 7:25. Then the video app flickered on. My wife stood next to her car in fading daylight. She kicked at the driver's side door lock with the heel of her boot. "That bastard is in our back yard! Colin!"

"I'm on it." My second in command relayed orders alerting every RCMP officer, plainclothes security and guard on The Hill. We ran down stairs, hallways and through doors into the cold reality of snow-dusted concrete and possible ambush.

"Where's the PM?" I shouted over my shoulder.

"Still in his office."

"Tell his detail to keep him there!"

"Done."

I redialed the most important contact in my life. "Jerilynn! Get in your car. Lock the doors!"

"Alec? What's wrong?"

"Do it!"

Men and women in uniforms detained and hustled staff and visitors indoors and took positions in the parking lot. I knew more would surround The Hill perimeter. My jurisdiction was secure. But bullets don't respect boundaries. *You've made this personal, dickhead,* I screamed in my head. *Hunting you down is now my job one.*

"Report!" I heard Colin's request for an update.

"No unusual activity, sir." "All clear here." Same response from every corner and checkpoint. We dodged between cars slotted in spaces reserved for high level government staff. I exhaled relief when I rounded the trunk of my wife's SUV. She'd followed orders. I tapped on the passenger's side window and got in the door she opened.

"What the hell is going on?"

I showed her the photos and video saved on my phone. "What's this?"

"Guns, money, politics and the lunatic fringe." The look in her eyes told me she'd put two and two together. I put my arms around her and tucked her head under my chin.

Colin tapped on the driver's side window. "Can you pop the hood?" he asked through the glass.

J-lynn pulled the release. Colin disappeared behind raised metal. His assessment of the reason my wife's car wouldn't start chilled me more than a blast of arctic air in Canadian winter.

"The battery cable has been cut."

My wife shivered. The cell phone rang.

"It's so entertaining to watch losers chase their tails," said unknown caller dickhead. "Tune in tomorrow in Toronto." The screen went dark.

"Son of a bitch."

"What did he mean by that?" The fright in J-lynn's voice and eyes frightened me.

"It's a long story, sweetheart. I'll tell you what I can on the way home." I got out of the disabled car and asked Colin to cover for me. "Can you finish up here?"

"Yeah, sure, no problem."

"Thanks, man. I owe you one."

§

Toronto's police chief and I go way back to RCMP cadet training. Rick Davis had traded the nomadic life of the detachment shuffle for a wife, kids and stability in his hometown. I wasn't surprised when I heard he'd elbowed his way to top cop of the department in record time.

"Hey, Alec!" Rick answered my call on the second ring. "You bored? Fed up writing parking tickets for diplomats?"

"Always the class clown." I smiled at the memory of an afternoon target practice at Depot Division in Regina. Rick smuggled opened lunch room ketchup packets in his pants pocket and reported his gun had misfired. He confessed to the prank before the medics were called. But our instructor was not amused. Privileges Rick didn't know he had got taken away. Washroom floors and urinals were spotless for weeks. "How the hell are you?"

"I'm still ass deep in projects on that fixer-upper we bought ten years ago and my youngest needs braces. But I can't complain. How about you?"

"Living the life with the love of my life."

Rick whistled through his teeth. "I saw a photo of her with the prime minister at a press conference. You are one lucky fucker, my friend."

"Don't I know it. I pinch myself every morning I wake up next to her."

"Any little ones?"

I'm not ruling it out. But I think my wife has. I swallowed to clear the sudden tightness in my throat. "No plans for a family just yet."

"I highly recommend parenthood. Best thing ever. But I'm betting this is more than a buddy call."

"I'm afraid so." Rick listened until I stopped talking. His low whistle confirmed the line was still open.

"So you think my department should be prepared for a major strike by these a-holes?"

"Edmonton, Winnipeg and Regina seem to have been spared. A hit on Canada's largest city and provincial capital sure as hell makes a statement and generates a shitload of media coverage."

"You're right about that. Any idea where this might go down?"

"Your guess is as good as mine. Probably a bar in a higher end neighborhood. Possibly near The Beaches or in Yorkville."

"That's what I was thinking. Thanks for the heads up Smart Alec."

I grinned at the nickname holdover from my academy days. "I hope you don't need it, my friend." Call ended, I stared at the cell phone and tried to coax the bastard out of the shadows with my mind. *This is between you and me. Stop fucking around. I'm here. Bring it.*

Chapter 16

Evan

The RCMP detail's choice of vehicle transported home three VIPs from Alta Vista Public School. I just happened to be along for the ride.

"Dad!" Isaac, our middle child and only son, encumbered by a bloated backpack, ran a crooked path from the school's main doors to my open arms.

"Hey, little man!" I scooped him up and held him as long as he and my back would let me. What had happened to the boy I carried on my shoulders? At nine years old, he was over half my height and less lanky and awkward than I had been at his age. "You're not so little anymore." I peeled the backpack off his shoulder and tossed it in on the backseat of the SUV. "Do you have a lot of homework?"

"Nah, I keep forgetting to take stuff out." He slid in and settled beside the load he'd carried.

"Daddy!" Corina, my seven-year-old ray of sunshine, called out the title I cherish most. Arms pumped and short legs churned, covered by layers that protected her from the cold. I caught her as she flung herself into my arms and wrapped hers around my neck. "Know what? My French teacher Mrs. Lamoureax says I'm her bestest student."

"Is that so?" I didn't have the heart to correct her English.

She closed her eyes. Her lips moved in practiced concentration. "*Mon jouet préféré est un lama violet.*" My favorite toy is a purple llama. The accents were a bit off on the syllables and her pronunciation of 'violet' was a shade too close to the English translation. "*C'est très bien,*" I said and rewarded her with a loud smack of a kiss on the cheek that I knew would make her giggle.

"Gabby! C'mon!" Isaac yelled to his sister through the still open car door. Our eldest child, born nine months to the day after Angeline and I exchanged wedding vows, broke away from a group of girls I presumed were classmates and friends. Her nonchalant measured walk toward the family reminded me of the pre-teen students in my classrooms a lifetime ago in Saskatoon.

"Hi Dad." She gathered the folds of her skirt in one hand, bracketed an armload of books with the other, and got in the SUV seat beside her brother. "Move over," she said to him, "*et je m'appelle Gabrielle.*"

"Maybe so, but gabby is what you are," Isaac grumbled. "All you do is talk, talk, talk."

I miss this. I buckled in Corina. "She said 'my name is Gabrielle,'" whispered my littlest angel.

"I know she did," I whispered back and got in the car door opened for me by my detail.

Twenty minutes and several games of I Spy later, the SUV glided to a stop in front of Rideau Cottage. Angeline stood on the porch, ready to gather our children and welcome home her too often absent spouse.

I lifted her chin with my fingertips and softly kissed lips glossed pale pink. Eyes the color of a mid-summer blue sky searched mine.

"Are you really here with us tonight? No distractions?"

"I promise I won't even answer the phone." My palms on her cheeks framed the alabaster beauty of her. My fingers parted the sleek softness of her long blonde hair. Her head tilted back, her eyes closed and we lost each other in a love and kiss so deep that all else fell away.

"What are we having for dinner?" Our son poked his head through the half-open front door. "I'm hungry."

Mutual smiles broke our kiss. I touched my forehead to hers. "I guess we'd better go in."

She reached for my hand and laced her fingers through mine. "Dinner. Homework. Then bedtime."

Angeline has always known how to heat up my anticipation.

§

Dinner was served an hour later. I'd forgotten how much fun it can be to simply reach in the cupboard and hand over dinner plates to Isaac, let Corina show me where to properly place the knife, fork and spoon and listen to Gabrielle's latest complaint about unfair class assignments. The teacher in me reacted to the eye roll and "Ugh, Shakespeare!" comment. I promised we'd discuss this after our family meal.

Pot roast, mashed potatoes and broccoli I had to coax Corina into eating by smothering the green with melted cheddar cheese filled our plates and stomachs. Isaac came up for air over his mother's delicious homemade cherry crumble.

"Dad. Do you ever talk to the president of China?" he asked.

"I have on occasion. Why do you ask?"

"Well, we're learning about China in school and we saw this documentary about the Great Wall of China. I got this idea on how the Chinese government could make a lot of money."

"Well, duh," Gabrielle responded. "I think they've got that figured out. China has way more money than Canada. Even more than the United States."

"Let's hear your brother out, please." That's my Angeline. Always the arbiter. "Go ahead, Isaac."

"Make it into a giant waterslide and charge people to go down it." My son leaned forward. His arms and torso swayed with the vision as if he were actually on a waterslide. "It's over twenty-one thousand kilometers long. That would be an incredible ride!"

I had to press the serviette to my mouth to keep from laughing out loud. His honest exuberance was endearing to the point of comical.

"You are such a dork," Gabrielle said.

"Gabrielle!" Angeline admonished our daughter again.

"If you can't say something nice, don't say anything at all," said the youngest philosopher at the table.

"That's right, Corina," Angeline said. "Thank you for that."

"What do you think, Dad?" Isaac asked.

"I'm not sure the Chinese would want one of the Seven Wonders of the World used as a waterslide," I responded. "But it is an interesting thought."

Once the dishes were cleared, the table and room converted to a study hall reserved for me and the reluctant student of The Bard. Gabrielle dropped The Complete Works of William Shakespeare on the table and flopped in the chair next to mine. "This is so ridiculous," she huffed. "It's not even English."

"On the contrary," I said. "The writings of Shakespeare influenced the development of the English language. His work standardized the rules of grammar. In fact, many of the common phrases we use today came from Shakespeare." I wasn't sure of her level of interest. But I definitely had her attention. "For example, 'heart of gold' came from Henry the Fifth. 'Break the ice' from Taming of the Shrew. 'Love is blind' from the Merchant of Venice'. 'Wild goose chase from Romeo and Juliet'."

"OK, Dad, I get the point." Gabrielle opened the thick volume to the bookmarked page. "That's what we're studying." She pointed to a section of text on the open page.

"Romeo's foreboding." I leaned back in the chair. "I know it well."

"That's the assignment."

Her eyes and hair are the same color as her mother, I thought. *I wonder if Angeline was as stubborn as Gabrielle at twelve going on thirteen.*

"Well, what does it mean?" she asked.

"Let's break it apart line by line." I recited the passage burned into my memory. "For my mind misgives. Put an i-n-g on the ending. Now what does it mean?"

"Misgivings?"

I nodded yes.

"I have misgivings about something."

"Exactly." I went on. "Some consequence yet hanging in the stars shall bitterly begin its fearful date with this night's revels."

"Ugh!"

"Think about it. What does consequence mean?"

"A result?"

"Yes. A result of an action that's 'yet hanging in the stars.' "

"Going to happen."

"Right. Keep going. Read it to me."

As my daughter read the next words, I felt the rush of satisfaction in watching the light bulb flicker and begin to glow. "A result of something that's going to happen tonight that may be bitter, meaning not so good."

"Now you've got it. What else?"

"And expire the term of a despised life closed in my breast by some vile forfeit of untimely death," she read out loud. "Romeo is afraid he's going to die?"

"Yes. And how does he think he's going to die?"

"I'm not sure." Gabrielle read the words again. "Not by natural cause or accident. Murder?"

"Possibly."

"Suicide?"

"Also a possibility. The next line tells the reader and the audience how Romeo feels about that possibility."

"But he that hath the steerage of my course direct my sail." Gabrielle tapped her fingernails on the table and looked out the window.

The light bulb glowed brighter.

"He accepts it because God has control of his life."

"Yes!"

"Now go write it down or do whatever you need to do and get ready for bed." Angeline stood behind me. Her fingers pressed and messaged the ache in my shoulders.

"OK. I get it. You want to be alone." Gabrielle closed the book of Shakespeare and tucked it under her arm. "Thanks, Dad."

"Goodnight, sweetheart." Her footsteps up the stairs meant the night was finally ours. I backed the chair away from the table. Angeline sat in my lap. "Isaac and Corina?" I asked between sweet, sensual touch and kiss.

"He's in his room. Door closed. Corina is asleep." She stood up and held out her hand. I took it and let her lead me up the stairs to our bedroom and behind our closed door.

My hands caressed the curves of her as she undressed in the dim light cast by a shaded lamp on the nightstand next to my side of the bed. Angeline's methodical removal of what I wore freed me to please her. She shivered as I knelt in worship of her, moaned with the first wave of tremble and release, sealed her lips over mine when I lifted her onto our bed and sighed at the finality of our joining.

The ringing phone pierced the golden haze of our afterglow.

"I'm not answering it." Truth be told, I was too spent at that moment to reach for it.

"Evan. You have to." I opened my eyes. She held the cell phone inches above my nose.

"Yes. What is it," I said.

"Sorry to bother you, Prime Minister."

Not half as sorry as I am, I wanted to say but of course did not. *My parliamentary secretary wouldn't call without good reason.*

"There's been an unfortunate incident at a bar in downtown Toronto." Kendra Greene reported the details of an argument over the handgun ban that turned violently ugly. At least two hundred people involved, twenty in hospital, three seriously injured. "The premier will be making a statement live on CBC News within the hour. I thought you needed to know."

"Thank you, Kendra."

"Again, my apologies for calling at such a late hour."

I tapped end call. The time on the phone display read 11:20.

"Are you going to call Jerilynn?" Angeline asked.

I thought about it and decided against it. "No. That can wait until morning." I set the cell phone face down on the night stand and turned out the light. "But this can't." I kissed my wife, deeply and passionately, until I felt the heat ignite between us again. "We can't."

Her body rose to entwine and meld with mine.

Chapter 17

Willie

The usual Saturday chores were finished on Friday. Willie had plans with Henry.

"I won't be home for dinner." Willie slapped the pockets of his well-worn jacket with the faded Maple Leafs logo. "Where are my keys?" he said under his breath. His mother rounded the corner from the kitchen. A set of keys dangled from a silver ring on her right pointer finger.

"Thanks, Mom." Willie took the keys from her, kissed her cheek, and noticed she no longer wore any makeup. Her pale cheeks seemed gaunter than usual, her misty blue eyes less bright. The naked nails she used to have manicured once a week picked at the crescent moon tear on the right shoulder of his jacket.

"I should sew that. Don't you have another coat to wear?"

"That's OK. It's been that way so long I don't even notice it anymore." Willie peeked through the front room curtains and waved at the driver of the car idling at the curb.

"Where are you going, Willie?" His mother's voice seemed to be getting smaller with age.

"With my friend Henry from work. See you later." He opened and quickly closed the front door against the cold. The soles of his boots stamped patterns in the snow as he trotted down the porch steps to the open side door of Henry's yellow pickup truck.

"Damn, it's freezin'. Get in!" Henry flipped the heat on full. Willie boosted himself up into the passenger seat, slammed the door and pressed his bare hands against the vent.

"Where are your gloves, man?" Henry asked.

"Lost them."

"Look in the glove compartment. I think I've got a spare pair."

"Much obliged." Willie slipped his fingers into the bulky red wool and pulled the fabric over his wrists. "So where is it?"

Henry gestured with his right thumb over his shoulder. "Behind the seat. Locked up, unloaded with the cable on and under the blanket. Out of sight."

"Your paperwork? The PAL, registration certificate and authorization of transport?"

"Right here." He opened the compartment in the console between their seats and tapped a closed envelope. "All the t's crossed and the i's dotted." Henry glanced at Willie and grinned. "You've been doing your homework."

"I watched training videos and read up on Canadian gun laws on the internet. I ran a ton of Call of Duty on my smartphone. For practice."

"Buddy, I gotta tell ya. Playing some game on a phone ain't nothin' like actually shooting a firearm."

§

Gravel crunched under the pickup's tires along the road leading into the parking lot of the single-story, flat metal roof building. Henry shifted the transmission and cut the engine. "Here we are. She's not much to look at. But we make do." Henry uncovered and lifted the hard sided case with two combination locks. "Grab the paperwork for me. They know me and I usually don't need it. But I always have it with me just in case."

Willie followed Henry through the door of the gun range, amazed at the number of people and greetings that welcomed his newfound friend. He stowed his coat in Henry's locker and walked alongside him toward his first experience firing bullets loaded in a real gun.

Henry showed Willie how to open the hard sided case. "Contrary to some popular belief, it's OK to keep ammo in with the firearm," Henry said. "But the gun can never be loaded in transport or storage at the registered home of the licensed owner."

"Yeah, I know that." Willie watched Henry unlock and remove the safety cable from the trigger. "Why the rubber grip?" he asked.

"Easier on my old hands." Henry nodded toward a pegged shelf along the side wall of the room fitted with Plexiglas stalls to accommodate up to a dozen sport shooters. "Grab us a couple of headsets." Willie hung a pair around his neck and brought the other to Henry.

"This is my baby." Henry lifted the gun from its case. "A Smith and Wesson 686. It'll shoot standard pressure .38 special or .357 magnum ammo. I prefer the 38 for target practice."

"Why?"

"Lower velocity but just as accurate."

"So the magnum ammo is more powerful?"

"Higher penetration properties, yeah. But you don't need to know all that just yet." He held out the unloaded gun. "Take it. Get a feel for it."

Willie nearly dropped the stainless steel weapon. "It's heavier than I thought," he said.

"It's solid all right but beautifully balanced. You'll appreciate the weight when you go to shoot. Good for taming the recoil." Henry loaded six bullets into the cylinder and covered his ears with the headset. "Watch my stance." He lifted the gun in his right hand, wrist supported by his left. Feet apart, staggered and angled one behind the other. "You might want to stand back."

Willie yelped and cupped his hands over his ears at the squeeze of the trigger. He shut his eyes at the flash spark. Acrid smoke from the barrel assaulted the hairs in his nostrils.

Henry lowered the gun and reloaded. "Headset," he said and pointed at the pair on his head.

Willie covered his ears as ordered.

"You ready?" Henry asked. He guided Willie on the position of his feet and correct way to hold the gun. "It's gonna kick up on you. So you better hold on. Take a breath. Aim. Squeeze the trigger."

The shock of power in his hands knocked Willie backward and out of stance. He totally missed the target.

"That's OK." Henry repositioned his shaken student. "Only thing to do is get back up on the horse. Take a breath. Aim. Squeeze."

Willie hit the target on the third try.

Henry whistled. "That's pretty good. You learn quick."

By the end of the third reload and the last of the ammunition, Willie's confidence and his aim had improved.

Henry slapped him on the back. "Wow. You're a natural, buddy. Were you pulling my leg?"

"What do you mean?"

"Those first couple of shots was way off. From then on you hit the target. That last shot was darn close to center." Henry snapped the cable over the trigger and put the gun safely away for transport. "You sure you've never used a firearm?"

"Positive."

"Well I'll be damned." He removed and handed his headset to Willie. "Put those back and let's go get something to eat. I'm starving."

Henry drove to a nearby diner famous for thick burgers and home-made fries. Hard case covered and doors securely locked, they took shelter from the cold at a window table within view of the pickup and ordered the house special.

"So what did you think of target practice, Willie my man?" Henry dipped fries in the pool of ketchup on his plate and stuffed the salted potato strips in his mouth.

"I really liked it. When can we go again?"

"Next Saturday if you want. Or any Saturday. Not much else to do on the weekends in winter other than watch the Maple Leafs lose by a goal and break our hearts again."

"Henry, I've got a question."

"Shoot. No pun intended."

"Let's say I had to defend myself. Where would I aim?"

Henry swallowed his big bite of burger. "Depends on the level of threat."

"What if the other guy has a gun?"

"Then you gotta make it count. If it's him or you, aim center mass."

"Center mass?"

"Yeah." Henry tapped the center of his chest. "Dead center. Go for the heart. The other guy won't know what hit 'em."

"Quick and painless."

"Pretty much. Unless you blow their head off, anywhere else hurts like hell. Burns like a son of a bitch and depending where the bullet enters the body a person can bleed out in less than five minutes. Nasty way to go." He mopped up the rest of the ketchup with the last of his burger. "Why do you want to know that?"

"Just curious. That's all." *Could I do that?* Willie tried to frame and shoot the video in his mind. The faceless threat approaching. The weight of the gun in his hand. The flash. The smell. The body jerking, convulsing, folding, falling. Blood staining the floor, spreading around and under the soles of his shoes. Looking down and into half-open eyes he knew. His father's mouth, open in one final silent scream. Remorse for the grief and pain that action would cause his mother twisted in his chest. *If I did do this, would I be glad he was gone?* Willie wasn't sure.

"Listen. I saw all the death I could stand on my tours of duty overseas. Even when it's you or them, taking a life tears you up. You're never the same." Henry picked up the bill from the table. "C'mon, buddy. I got beers in the fridge. Let's go back to my place and watch the Leafs lose."

"I'm good with that. Except for the Leafs losing."

Willie couldn't remember the last time he'd actually enjoyed his day off.

Chapter 18

March ~ Alec

All the Saturday morning news feeds led with details of the late Friday night bar fight that spilled out onto and disrupted traffic along Yonge Street. Toronto police had spent the weekend tracking down and interviewing witnesses. Despite the size and scope of the incident, no arrests had been made. Everyone involved, from the bouncer who tried to break it up and got his leg broken to three University of Toronto graduate students hit by beer bottles while on their way out the door, told the same account of how the fight started. Loud and vulgar protests over the ban the handgun amendment to the federal government's gun control law. But no one knew who threw the first punch.

I left a message on Rick's cell phone. Toronto's top cop called me on Sunday night. "Sorry, man," I said. Anything I can do to help?"

"You tell me, chief superintendent on Parliament Hill. We're chasing ghosts here. Whoever it is went out of their way to hurt people who were minding their own business for no apparent reason than to make a lot of noise and leave a big mess."

"Did I hear right? Over two hundred eye witnesses and no arrests?"

"Yeah, it's the damndest thing. Whoever started it came in, blended in with the crowd, and got out when the shit hit the fan."

"So no descriptions. But everyone agrees an argument over the handgun ban lit the fuse."

"That's right. What's really weird about it is not that many people squawked when the Liberals promised to support municipal laws that would ban handguns. Whether the amendment passes or not, Toronto's mayor and city council were all for making handguns illegal in our city. It's going to be a bitch to enforce. But in the long run, saving the lives of civilians and cops is what it's all about. No argument from where I sit. Anything else from the unknown caller?"

"Nothing. I've gone over every frame of CCTV footage from on and around The Hill the day before, the day of and the day after I called to warn you. Studied that shit until my eyes crossed."

"You said the battery cables were cut on your wife's car."

"That's right."

"CCTV didn't pick up anybody messing around with her car?"

"Whoever it was knew how to pop a hood without breaking into the car or setting off the security alarm. All I got are skinny legs in tight jeans and an oversized parka. The angle of the camera wasn't the best. That's been corrected."

"That's a pain in the ass. You've got about as much to go on as I do."

"I got a hunch the person in the parka isn't the unknown caller. He wouldn't risk getting caught on camera or any other way."

"Any possible suspects from your cell phone contact list?"

"Only J-lynn, the commissioner, my operations director, the office manager and now you have this number."

"That's a pretty short list. Could it be in your personnel file?"

"It is an RCMP issue cell phone, so, yes, it would be. But those numbers are not written down anywhere. They're confidential and protected."

"No device is completely hack-proof, my friend."

"Thanks for giving me yet another reason to get pissed off."

Rick's all-in laugh always made me smile. "Thank you. I needed that."

The glass of Malbec and the woman who brought it to me was what I needed. J-lynn sat sidesaddle on the arm of my recliner. I groaned in pleasure at her caress along and under my shirt collar.

"Weekends aren't long enough," she said. "Especially when they're longer."

"Are you OK with going back to The Hill?" My wife had taken a rare personal day off on Friday. I insisted. She didn't resist.

"I admit that I was creeped out a bit. But government and life goes on."

"So does the pursuit of criminals and justice." I tapped my glass with hers. "That's especially annoying when the clues don't add up."

"The devil is in the details and I'm especially good with those. Let me help."

"I need all the help I can get." I sipped the wine and stroked her thigh. "The dots between Victoria, Saskatoon and Toronto should connect. But they aren't. There has to be a reason that those three targets have been hit so hard."

"Two are provincial capitals."

"But why skip three others?"

"I see your point and problem." My wife swirled the wine in her glass. "Saskatoon is plain and placid. I was there once with the prime minister a couple of months or so after he was sworn in. We visited the school where he taught sixth grade. The photo of him with his first class is framed and hanging on the wall in his old classroom."

The lines between the dots were coming into sharper focus. But where does it lead? "J-lynn, isn't Victoria the prime minister's hometown?"

"Yes. His Dad was mayor there then MP for the Victoria riding before he was prime minister."

"Has he ever lived in Toronto?"

"He might have but I don't think so."

"Has anyone in his family lived there?"

"That's Angeline's hometown. She graduated from the University of Toronto. Her parents live in Yorkville."

Holy fuck! I reached for my cell phone and redialed Rick. "Where along Yonge Street is that bar that was trashed? Anywhere near U of T and Yorkville?"

"Yeah. A half dozen blocks or so in between. Why? Are you on to something?"

"I might be. Not sure yet. But when I am I'll let you know."

J-lynn took the glass of wine from my hand. "You're shaking."

"I'm thinking."

"What are you thinking?"

"That son of a bitch unknown caller is leaving a trail for me to follow."

I couldn't and didn't want to tell where I thought it might end.

Chapter 19

Ottawa

The big man booked every room in the guest house through the end of April. He paid in cash. The base of operations was adequate. The quiet working class neighborhood near the more affluent Vanier riding represented by the Liberal leader of government situated him within close proximity to his intended victims. A brisk fifteen minute walk away from the residence of Alec and Jerilynn Martin. Two kilometers from Parliament Hill. The guest house provided complimentary off-street parking for the nondescript white panel van he'd modified to hide and transport contraband.

The thump and drag of feet in heavy boots echoed in the staircase to the modest top floor suite he'd occupied. He deflected a raised fist punched through the room's open door.

"Where the fuck were you?" Troy's other arm was bound to his body by a makeshift sling. Butterfly bandages on a clotted gash over his blackened left eye held the edges of the wound together.

"Get your ass in here!" The big man grabbed the collar of Troy's coat, pulled him through and closed the door. "And keep your voice down."

Troy jabbed his forefinger into the big man's chest. "You agreed to be there. Back us up in Toronto in case it got ugly. It got more than ugly. We got our asses kicked!"

"You had six members, two more than the other strikes."

"We needed more! The cops were everywhere! If I hadn't torched more cars, we all wouldn't have got out of there. It's like they were ready for us. Like they knew we were coming." The muscles in his arm flexed with his clenched fist. "What did you say to that Mountie?"

"That's not your concern," the big man hissed through clenched teeth.

"The fuck it isn't!" Troy cradled his injured left arm with his right. "This isn't the worst of it. Tucker's jaw is busted. He's out. I had to threaten to do worse to that weasel Duvall to shut him up. He's asking whose car it was he fucked with. I didn't know what the hell he was talking about. But I bet you do."

The big man kicked the leg of a straight-backed chair near the window overlooking the street. "Sit down. Take a load off." He opened the door of the mini-fridge. "You want a beer?"

Troy stayed where he was. "I'm not gonna drink with you. You betrayed us. You don't give a shit if our guns are taken away. You're using us to thumb your nose at the RCMP and play head games with that Mountie."

"You're right." Foam oozed over the top of the can the big man opened. He slurped the suds and gulped the beer. "No matter how the vote goes, I'll keep my guns. I don't give a shit if that's legal or not. But you do. So I made a deal with that devil who supplied us with government documents and a butt load of cash so we can both get what we want." He took another can of beer from the fridge. "Alec Martin is where and what I was supposed to be. He lied and took that away from me. So I'm going to pay him back and in the process put to death a traitor you and I both despise."

The tab he pulled opened the can he handed to Troy. "Drink your beer and we'll talk about the hit in Gatineau."

Chapter 20

Alec

I'd mentally ignored the warnings from colleagues in law enforcement about the numbing effect of trading boots on the ground police work for a move up the ranks to administration. Don't lose your cop sense in those piles of paperwork, they'd said.

First thing Monday morning, I put in a call to RCMP head office. "Commissioner, we need to talk."

"Can this wait until our regular meeting on Wednesday?"

"No. It can't. I have reason to believe there is a substantial threat to Parliament Hill and the safety of the prime minister."

"What is the nature of the threat?"

"I'd prefer we discuss this in person."

"Very well. My office."

"On my way."

The grumble of discontent rolled through the ranks the day the prime minister announced Chris Burke's appointment as commissioner. Another token woman where she doesn't belong. Her record of service isn't up to par. Deputy Commissioner Fill in the Blank would have been a better choice. By the end of her first year, she silenced the naysayers with a no exceptions to the new rules policy that rooted out systemic racism and added layers of protection and routes to report abuses and grievances for indigenous and marginalized Canadians. While she and I had not always agreed, I respected her open door willingness to listen. I needed her to do exactly that now.

"Come in Chief." Commissioner Burke trimmed titles and words used in the interest of brevity, a trait I also admired. "What have you got?"

I flipped through pages of facts with pertinent points of dates in reverse concern from the recent episode in Toronto to the violence in Victoria two weeks into the New Year. She listened, jotted down notes as I spoke and asked questions when she had them. Broad shoulders squared under the uniform decorated by highest rank. "What is your assessment?" she asked.

"The pattern and repetition of reports suggest the incidents are related to the handgun ban amendment with the intent to delay or disrupt debate and a final vote in the House of Commons."

"I would agree."

"I believe escalated violence of the attacks in Victoria, Saskatoon and Toronto are in some way linked to and could threaten the prime minister."

"Based on?"

"The specific locations." I explained my theory and suspicions. The commissioner reviewed what she'd written down and sat back in her chair. "What would be your recommended course of action?"

"Increase the security detail around the prime minister."

"Immediately, yes. And?"

"I need permission to expand my involvement in this investigation beyond Parliament Hill. Commissioner, whoever called and texted my cell phone is closely involved with the people responsible for this threat. It's reasonable to assume he knows me. He made that clear when he sent photos of my wife outside our home and in The Hill parking lot where her car was deliberately disabled."

"Permission granted. Work smart, Chief. Don't work alone. Assign an officer to have your back every step of the way."

"Thank you, Commissioner."

§

The semi-slick mix of ice pellets and the crusty slush of half-melted dirty snow crackled under my shoes. I scraped the car windows clear and slid under the steering wheel as the cell phone in my pants pocket vibrated its need to be answered.

"What is your location and ETA at the townhome I'm parked in front of that is dark and apparently unoccupied at the moment."

I marveled at the intensity of my love for the woman I'd marry again and the sudden jab of fear for her safety. "I'm about to pull out of the parking lot. Stay in your car and keep the doors locked until I get there."

"Why? Do you know something I don't? Or are you just being paranoid?"

"The latter. Humour me, sweetheart."

"I could go for take out."

If that dickhead is there, he'll follow you. The scenarios on what could go wrong flashed behind my eyes like a macabre newsreel. "I'll come up with something for dinner. Please, just stay where you are. I'll be there in ten minutes."

The knot in my gut untied when I parked behind J-lynn's car and saw that she was in it. With my arm around her waist, I walked us to and through our front door.

"Do you mind telling me what that was all about? I know why I was late. The gun ban amendment is teetering on the brink of report stage out of committee. What's your excuse?" To everyone else, my cop face signals a 'don't ask because I won't tell' position. My wife sees right through the hard set mask. That's when the probe intensifies. "OK, out with it, Alec.

"Well." I grabbed hangers from the closet and hung up our coats. "The good news is the commissioner has ordered extra detail around your boss. The bad news is why he needs it." I told her what I could without compromising the scope of the investigation.

"To review, just so I've got this straight. The battle in the Toronto bar last Friday is one link in a petty crime to violent incident diversion chain that stretches back to Victoria and whoever posted those photos of me and vandalized my car is part of that chain. That threat is circling Parliament Hill and the prime minister is the likely target."

"We don't know that for sure." I rested my hands on her shoulders and massaged muscles tight from tension. She groaned in stress-release pleasure. "But it is a reasonable conclusion. I recommended the increase in security and the commissioner agreed." I kissed her forehead. "I guess you won't need that white lie."

Green eyes that reminded me of the glassy calm ocean off Carter's Beach before the tide rolls in stared into mine. "I know you're not telling me everything and I get it. You can't. Just promise me a heads-up if and when I need one."

"You know I will." I kissed her lips, light and sweet, with the promise of more. "That's my job."

Chapter 21

Evan

Eight years as prime minister witnessing partisan pomposity and battling relentless bickering in the House of Commons had come down to this.

Dave Getti, my cabinet minister of public safety and sponsor of the handgun ban amendment, scrubbed long fingers over a day old growth of stubble above and below his deep frown. "The Tories have really rallied the opposition on this one," he told me. "They are insisting that the firearm buyback provision has to be tacked on to the amendment."

I tapped the retracted tip of the pen in my hand on the desk. "What are we talking about here? The assault weapon buyback is already in the budget."

"They want to pull it out and add in the costs of the handgun buyback."

"And their strategy is, oh let me guess, argue taxpayer sticker shock in the time of burgeoning post-pandemic budget deficit."

"That's about it."

"How many NDP and Bloc Quebecois MPs are in this corner?"

"All of them. And they've recruited Vincent Lockwood, a Liberal on Poirier's committee."

Thunder in my ears signaled the initial stage of blood boil. I leaned back in the chair and breathed. "What do they want to move out of it?"

"They're not talking just yet. That may take a while."

I stood up and paced the room. To hell with anger management. "Dave, we don't have the luxury of time. Third reading is scheduled a month from today. The amendment was referred to committee after the second reading. Buyback exceeds the scope of the amendment. The Speaker could rule the changes out of order and with good reason."

"I know that, Prime Minister." Dave stressed his commitment to succeed with the fleshy hammer of his loosely-clenched fist on his knee. "Everyone has an angle to play in this game. I promise you I'll find out what theirs is. We'll get this amendment through and on to royal assent."

"I know you will. Whatever I can do, just tell me. We need this to happen. If we miss this chance there may never be another."

"Understood."

"Thank you, Dave." I walked him to and through my office door and called my chief of staff.

"Yes, Prime Minister?" she answered.

"Can you clear your afternoon schedule?"

"Of course. What do you need?"

I closed the door behind me and leaned hard against it. "A friend."

Chapter 22

Jerilynn

Our code for 'help me' changed whatever else I had planned. I closed up shop, told my executive assistant that I was gone for the day, and climbed the spiral stairway. The door to his office was closed. An ominous sign as he obviously knew I was on my way. I knocked. The door opened. He had his coat on.

This was serious.

"Let's get out of here."

"And go where?"

"Harrington Lake. We'll have an hour or so to talk before Angeline and the children get there." We walked side-by-side to the waiting RCMP vehicle and detail. He briefed me on where we stood with the handgun ban bill amendment during the thirty minute drive from Parliament Hill to the PM's summer residence and all-season retreat.

I wasn't surprised and had actually anticipated Lockwood's difference of opinion with the prime minister and his party. "He's been badgering me for a slot on your schedule since first reading in November. I met with Lockwood after holiday break. He's concerned about the cost of buyback. But his main objection is enforcement. We discussed the options and reached a compromise that he could push through even if the committee chair objected."

The prime minister's half smile held no humour. "Kingston Poirier rears his Tory head yet again."

"Lockwood told me he met with Poirier before Parliament reconvened. He insisted the amendment had to be placed on the agenda for second reading."

"Were any of the other committee members present at this meeting?"

"No. Only Poirier's assistant. Lockwood said Poirier had asked him to be there to take notes."

"I'm familiar with his tactics. I'm sure Poirier called a one-on-one with every member of his committee. Lockwood wants to meet with me, fine. Set it up on both our schedules. We need to know where he stands and what Poirier is up to. Just how far is the official opposition's shadow public safety minister willing to go to get whatever it is he wants?"

Urban sprawl ended with forest reclaimed from farmland that surrounded the property's main cottage. Here in this place of solitude where he'd learned as a boy to swim and fish we followed Evan's rule. No titles. Formality and protocol shed. Friends sharing confidentialities and consequences no one else in our lives could know or understand. I sat on the family-sized sofa facing the windowed overlook and marveled at the mist on the lake streaked golden with the slant of rays from a setting sun.

I heard the refrigerator door open in the kitchen nearby. "What's your pleasure, *mon amie?*" he called out. "Beer? Wine? Something else?"

"I'd love a glass of chardonnay."

"You got it."

Cupboards opened and glasses rattled. I heard the distinctive pop of a cork pulled from the neck of a bottle and his footsteps across the floor. He sat beside me. I took the glass of wine he'd poured and savoured the buttery taste. "This is lovely. But why are we here? What's up?"

He stared out at the ripple and swell of waves reaching to catch the fading light of day. "We've been through so much together over the last eight years and done good work. But if handguns are still legal when the next prime minister is sworn in, I will have failed. Miserably, totally and utterly failed. We're here so that I can tell you why." He tipped back the glass and gulped the wine as though he needed it to finish what he'd started to say. He set the empty glass on the long low table in front of us. "I've never told anyone this. Not even Angeline."

I sipped my drink and waited in silent privilege for the reason and story my boss and friend had kept hidden.

"I had a student in the sixth grade class my first year teaching in Saskatoon. Brilliant boy. First Nations. Spoke unintelligible English and not a word of French. His teachers had given up on him. He was belligerent, they told me. Uncooperative. He hadn't been tested but they'd concluded that if he were his IQ and aptitude results would be low. But I saw a spark in him, a yearning to learn. I was determined to find a way to reach him. So I asked him to teach me his language. Through that common connection he learned mine. From that point on, he soaked up knowledge like a sponge. It was like he'd been lost in the wilderness, couldn't find clean water and was suddenly handed a full canteen of it. I helped him fill out and submit the applications. He was accepted at three universities. On the first day of his senior year, he brought his brother to my classroom. 'Do for him what you did for me, Mr. Reid, he said.'

"Two weeks into the second semester, his brother went home and found him. Their father's gun safe was open. The loaded handgun beside the body was missing two bullets. One had been fired into the framed family portrait blown to pieces on the floor. It had been hanging on the wall in the living room. The other bullet was in Keme's brain."

I gasped and grasped his hand. "Oh, Evan. How awful." At that moment, those were the only words I had.

He went on. "His brother dropped out of school. The family moved away and left their possessions behind. They couldn't even go back in that house." He sank back into the cushions and rubbed his eyes dry. "What a waste. Maybe it would have happened anyway. Maybe his pain was too much to live with and he would have found another way to end it. But if that handgun hadn't been there maybe Keme would have lived. Gone to university. Gone on to accomplish great things. His brother had the same spark. Did it go out, too? I'll never know."

He squeezed my hand and held on. "But know this, Jerilynn. If it's the last thing I do, handguns will be illegal in Canada. I owe that to Keme and every other man, woman and child that has died from a bullet fired from a handgun, whether their cause of death was self-inflicted, accidental or deliberate. Guns that are only used to kill people have no place in this remarkable caring country of ours."

The soft tick of a clock counted the passing seconds in otherwise silent and subdued surroundings. "You know I'll do everything and anything I can to get that amendment through to royal assent," I assured him. The somber mood lifted with the spill of switched on overhead light and the rapid tap of child-size shoes across the floor.

"Daddy!"

Everything changed with that single word. Evan stood and crossed past me to gather up his daughter and smother her with kisses. His joy at her giggles transformed him. All that mattered at that moment was the child in his arms.

"I got an A on my math test!"

"You did?"

Curls bobbed on her forehead when she nodded 'yes'. "And I learned about spiders in science class today."

"Can you tell me that in French?" he asked.

Her nose wrinkled in concentration. "Maybe."

"We'll do it together," he said and helped her through the translation word-by-word. I had forced myself to become fluent in Canada's other official language. If I'd had a teacher like Evan, maybe the struggle wouldn't have been so frustrating.

The next set of footsteps trudged ahead of a steady scrape of something dragged across the floor. "Why do I have to carry everybody else's stuff?" The blonde-haired boy with dark eyes like his father's let go the straps of a small backpack. The sparkly pink and white fairy princess imprinted on its front tumbled to lie face down on the floor.

"Isaac, take the cloth bag at the front door to the kitchen, please," a voice I recognized as his mother's called out.

"Ugh!" The boy stripped off the straps of the backpack on his shoulders and dropped the plain brown canvas bundle next to the fairy princess.

Angeline thanked Isaac on his way to help out as requested. "Hello, my love," she said to her husband and lightly kissed his lips.

"Where's Gabrielle?" he asked her. The front door slammed in response.

"I'm missing Jenna's party because we had to come here." The adolescent version of Angeline broadcast her displeasure and disappointment through every possible position of negative body language. Arms crossed. Head down. Feet poised for exit. But her delicate beauty shone through the pout.

"Manners, please," Evan said. "We have a guest."

"Oh, Jerilynn." Angeline's look of surprise quickly turned apologetic. "How rude of us."

"That's OK." I fished out the cell phone from my jacket pocket. "I should be going."

"Would you like to stay for dinner?" Angeline asked.

"We're gonna have macaroni and cheese!" Corina said.

"I'm not." Gabrielle hiked up the bag slung over her shoulder and stomped down a hallway.

"Gabrielle!" Evan set Corina on her feet and strode off in the direction of his oldest daughter's exit.

Corina climbed up on the couch cushion next to mine. "Do you like macaroni and cheese, Jerilynn?"

I smiled at her puffy-cheeked cherubic face. "Yes, I do. But I have to go home to my husband."

"Does he like macaroni and cheese?" she asked.

Angeline sat next to her daughter. "Well, I guess we know what's on the menu for tonight." She brushed Corina's curls from her forehead and looked over the top of her head at me. "You are both more than welcome to have dinner with us."

She'd extended an invitation I couldn't and really didn't want to refuse. "I'll call Alec." I got up from the couch and walked to the far side of what I'd describe as an ample but inviting space. Seating areas had been staged around a stone fireplace and windows with calming views of placid nature.

"What's up, gorgeous?" he answered on the second ring tone. "Where are you?"

"Harrington Lake with the Reid family. We've been invited to dinner."

"Oh for fuck's sake."

"Before you say anything else, I haven't volunteered you. But …"

"You want me to play chef."

"In a word, yes."

He snorted. "What the hell am I going to cook for the prime minister and his wife? Don't they have three kids?"

"You know they do. C'mon Alec. It's a fully stocked kitchen. I'm sure you'll come up with something. I'll make it easy for you. Their seven-year-old daughter wants macaroni and cheese."

"That's actually one of my kid-friendly specialties. My sister's crew can't get enough of it." He hesitated. But I knew he would agree. "OK. You owe me big time, beautiful."

"I love you."

"Yeah, I love you, too. See you in twenty."

Either he's closer than I thought or he doesn't have to worry about getting a speeding ticket. On my return to give Angeline an answer, I noticed Isaac had slumped in a chair near his mother and sister. Thumbs on the cell phone in his hands typed out a text message. Evan and Gabrielle were still missing in action.

"Alec is on his way," I crossed my fingers to tell a harmless lie, "and he's offered to make dinner."

"That's very generous of him but ..," Angeline protested.

Her son cut into the conversation. "Men don't cook," he said.

"Mine does," I replied. "He's an excellent cook."

Gratitude and relief accompanied Angeline's smile. "Well, then. The least we can do is get the kitchen and table ready," she told her children. We all pitched in. Alec arrived as the last place was set at the table. Evan met him at the door.

"Good evening, Prime Minister," I heard my husband say. I'd forgotten to tell him about Evan's rule.

"Here, I'm just Evan."

The response I expected.

Corina skipped ahead of me. "They're staying for dinner, Daddy."

She pointed at Alec. "And he's gonna cook."

Evan's lips lifted in an amused half-smile. He looked from Alec to me. "What's this about? Other duties as assigned?"

"Jerilynn can be very persuasive," Alec said.

"So I've noticed on numerous occasions." I followed the two most important men in my life into the kitchen.

"Whoa." Alec stood in awe before the six burner range. "I have got to get me one of these."

"That's too big for our kitchen," I said.

"I'd make it fit," Alec replied.

"I've only ever used two or maybe three burners at one time." Angeline set a large wooden cutting board on the counter next to the range top. "This is such a treat. Other than caterers, I can't remember the last time someone else prepared our meal."

"I'm happy to do it, Mrs. Reid."

She shook her head and flattened her palm on her chest. "I'm Angeline." She draped her arm across her son's shoulders. "This is Isaac and I believe you've already met Corina."

The littlest Reid tugged on Alec's shirt sleeve. "Do you know how to make macaroni and cheese?" she asked.

He looked down at her and grinned. "I certainly do. I have a special recipe."

Gabrielle entered and ignored us. She walked a deliberate path to and opened the refrigerator.

"That's Gabby Grumpy Pants," Isaac said.

The refrigerator door slammed closed. Gabrielle stood with her fists on her hips. "You are such a jerk."

98

"Gabrielle." I sensed no anger in Evan's stern reprimand. "I thought we had resolved this."

"Make him apologize, Dad!"

"Isaac. Apologize to your sister."

"Aw, Dad .."

"Apologize."

His shoulders lifted in an insincere shrug. "OK. I'm sorry, Grumpy Pants."

Gabrielle stomped her foot. "Dad!"

Evan's chin dropped to his chest. "Sometimes there's no negotiating with the opposition." He beckoned to his children and pointed toward the intended elsewhere in the cottage destination. "I think it's time for a time out."

"I didn't do anything!" Corina complained.

"Then you and I will have time together before dinner." He took her hand and shepherded Gabrielle and Isaac out and away from the main living space.

Alec chose a bottle of Chablis from the rack in the wine cooler and held it out for Angeline's approval. "Oh yes, thank you," she said and took the full glass poured from the bottle he'd uncorked. He poured another glass and handed it to me. "Ladies, go relax and enjoy. Dinner will be ready in about thirty minutes."

We settled on the couch and looked out over a smooth lake beneath a sky full of stars. Angeline sipped her wine and rested her head back on the cushion. "You don't know much I needed this."

"I'm sure it's not easy being a single parent so much of the time."

"More difficult than I thought it would be. I try not to burden Evan with my frustrations. He's certainly got enough of his own. Neither of us planned on his being prime minister and definitely not for this long." She glanced toward the kitchen. "Maybe I should see if your husband needs any help."

"Believe me. He doesn't. When he's out of uniform, he's in his element in a kitchen."

"Is that his way of relieving stress?"

"Yes and no. He just loves to cook."

"Evan burns scrambled eggs. You're lucky."

"I know I am." I grinned at the mental image of the Prime Minister of Canada scraping a pan of blackened whites and yolks into the garbage.

Angeline nodded toward the lake. "That's where Evan goes. The longer he's out there with a fishing rod the greater is his need to get relief. He tells me what he can. But I know he can't tell me everything. You and Alec are probably up against similar barriers."

"We are. But we've adjusted. We each have our ways of blowing off steam."

"Ah." Her sideways glance indicated understanding. "So you've witnessed that side of my husband as well."

"He does have a temper."

"So I've heard but not seen. We haven't had a serious argument of any sort in our fifteen years together and he's never been angry with the children."

"Hasn't he been on Parliament Hill since you got married?"

Angeline nodded. "Our wedding was in July. Evan won his riding in October. Gabrielle was born the following April. Isaac arrived a month before the election my husband and his party won again."

"I remember Corina was a newborn when Evan was sworn in as prime minister. How have you coped?"

"I've had help from someone who has been there and done this."

"Celine."

"I honestly don't know how I could have kept it together without her. She's always been there at exactly the right time, just when I've, when we've, needed her most."

Activity from the kitchen indicated dinner was about to be served. Angeline summoned her family and we all sat down to a heaping bowl of pasta carbonara and macaroni and cheese ala Alec.

"This is the bestest I've ever had!" Corina finished her first helping and sunk the spoon for more into her favorite dish.

"Incredible." Evan twirled the spaghetti with his fork. "This is absolutely on a par with a state dinner prepared by top chefs in Rome."

I couldn't believe it! Alec actually blushed! "You flatter me and I accept the praise."

Evan watched his son devouring a second plate of pasta. "Will you be coming up for air anytime soon, Isaac?"

"This is so good," Isaac spoke through a mouthful of food. "Sorry," he muttered from behind his napkin.

"It is delicious and of course I must have your recipes," Angeline said to my husband.

"Baking has recipes. Cooking doesn't. But I'll do my best," Alec said.

"Maybe you can teach my Dad to cook, "Isaac said. "The last time he made us kids lunch, the hot dogs blew up in the microwave."

The contagious ripple of laughter exploded like the doomed wieners Isaac described. Everyone shared in the humour of Evan's kitchen ineptitude except for the glum Gabrielle.

Her father called her out. "Gabrielle. We're all waiting to hear from you."

She put down her fork. "Thank you for making dinner for us. I enjoyed the pasta very much." She patted her mouth with her napkin. "*Puis-je être excusée?*" May I be excused?

"*Nettoyez votre vaisselle,*" Angeline responded. Clear your dishes.

Gabrielle stacked her plate and utensils and took what she'd used to the kitchen on the way to what I assumed was her bedroom.

Angeline sighed. "I would apologize for my daughter but I, too, have been a twelve year old girl."

Table cleared, Isaac said goodnight and went to his room. Evan carried a sleepy little girl to her bed. Angeline and I finished the bottle of Chablis and chatted in the kitchen while the men conversed on the couch.

"So, that wasn't so bad, was it?" I asked Alec during the moonlit ride back home.

"Not at all," my husband said. "I actually had a good time." Most of the windows along the street where we live were dark and our neighbors likely asleep at the midnight hour. Alec parked the car at the curb and turned off the engine. "Evan. The prime minister."

"What about him?"

"He's not what I expected."

"What did you expect?"

"I don't know. I mean, sitting on the couch. We talked about fishing and hockey. He's just a regular guy."

"He is a regular guy and an extraordinary man." I released the seat belt and kissed the one and only love I'd ever known. "So are you."

Getting ready for bed required taking off our clothes which of course led to lovemaking as fresh and spontaneous as our first night of playful passion. I snuggled against my partner for life. "I'm not sure how long this will last."

"We're in this forever."

"I know we are. But I think the prime minister has had enough. Once this handgun ban amendment is law, I wouldn't be surprised if he decides to retire."

"And do what?"

"Teach. Take the single parent pressure off Angeline. Be with his family. Stay home with his kids."

"And what will you do, Madame Chief of Staff?"

Should I tell him what I really want? I teased him with a slight tug from my fingers and light scrape of my fingernails. "Maybe I'll have a baby and stay home. What do you think of that idea, Chief Superintendent?"

His kiss and caress stopped. My heart nearly did. He rolled over to his side. I couldn't read an emotion from the look in his eyes. "Are you serious?"

Do I tell him how long I've been trying to conceive? That I'm afraid of what could happen if we can't? "I am if you are." The long seconds of silence were suffocating. I took a breath to break it. "Alec, tell me what you're thinking."

103

The gentleness of his touch opened all our possibilities. "I think if I'm going to be this family's sole source of income, I'd better put in for a promotion."

I crossed my fingers for luck as his body covered mine.

Chapter 23

April ~ Alec

The first Tuesday morning of a new month delivered a red flag warning notice that I had been expecting but never wanted to see.

From: Commanding Officer National Division RCMP Headquarters Ottawa

To: Chief Superintendent Alec Martin Director of Parliamentary Protective Service

Subject: Incursion probability alert

Ottawa Police advise unusually high number of demonstration applications submitted regarding protests of handgun ban amendment to Bill C-71. All requests for permits to protest in proximity of Parliament Hill on Wednesday 19 April.

Repeat code activity on social media related to anti-government pro-gun network traced to presumed aliases provided as permit applicant contacts.

And there it is. These slimy bastards were planning to use the cover of legal protest to disrupt the third reading debate and vote. The when and where of their attack was no surprise. Neither was the why. Nailing down the who and how could keep what from happening.

The outer office buzzed in before I could call Colin into my office. "Police Chief Davis on line one for you, sir."

"Thank you, Grace." I switched desk phone lines. "Yeah, Rick. What's up?"

"Grab the keys to a marked unit, light it up and get here pronto."

"What have you got?"

"A bird that's ready to sing about who started that bar brawl. I think you might want to hear the lyrics."

"I'm on my way." I grabbed my uniform jacket and required gear for a road trip, closed the office door behind me, and caught Colin outside his office. "You're with me."

"Where to?"

"Toronto."

§

Interrogation rooms strike fear in the hearts and minds of those who suffer from claustrophobia. I am not one so afflicted. But I sensed the bouncer with his leg in a cast was desperate to get this interview over and out into the overcast afternoon sooner and not a minute later than necessary. "Duane, this is Chief Superintendent Alec Martin and Operations Officer …"

"Yeah, I get it, RCMP, probably national out of Ottawa." Duane with no last name fidgeted in the metal chair. "You got a pencil? I need something to scratch the itch under this damn plaster."

Rick pulled a pen from his shirt pocket. Duane shoved the pen between his thigh and the top of the cast below a ragged cut of what had been a full leg of baggy canvas work pants. He grimaced then low moaned in relief. "This wasn't supposed to happen."

I sat across from Duane in an identically ugly and likely uncomfortable metal chair across a gouged up fake wood table. "Enlighten me. What wasn't supposed to happen?"

"This!" Duane indicated the cast. "I work construction. Now I can't work my day job or weekends at the bar. All because I took a couple hundred dollar bills to hold a table as a favor for a couple of guys."

"Are they friends of yours?"

"Hell no! I'd never seen them before. They came to the bar about ten minutes before we opened. Asked me to reserve a table in the back next to the fire exit. I told them that we didn't hold tables. That's when they slipped me the two hundred bucks. Said they'd be back at ten. I took the chairs away from the table around 9:30 or so. Put a tray of dirty glasses on it to keep people from asking to sit down. They showed up at the door on time. I took them back to the table. They told me not to bother when I went to move the tray and get the chairs. Five minutes later, BOOM!" Duane clapped his hands together and spread his fingers apart. "Fists and bottles and chairs are flying. The fire alarm goes off. Some asshole must have hit the crash bar on the back door. Another asshole broke a chair over my leg and busted it in two places." Duane glanced around his confines like an anxious animal in a trap. He wiped the sweat from his forehead and upper lip. "Can I get some water?" he asked.

Rick left and came back with a paper cup probably filled at the cooler. Duane gulped every drop.

"Tell them what you told me about the hospital visit," Rick said.

"Yeah, I was getting to that." Duane crushed the paper cup in his fist. "These guys came to see me the day after surgery. Offered to pay me big bucks to keep my mouth shut. Said they'd cover whatever extra medical costs I had, pay for physiotherapy and give me double my lost wages for time off work. The envelope that was shoved under the door to my apartment this morning had two thousand dollars in it and this note." Duane unfolded the piece of paper he'd removed from the front pocket of his hacked up pants and shoved it across the table.

"Paid in full," I read out loud.

"That's some bullshit!" Duane wiped away the sweat again. "That's less than I make in a good week on a construction site!"

"Were the guys at the hospital the same guys you let into the bar?"

107

"One of them was. He was banged up. Had a gash on his forehead and a puffed out black eye. His arm was in a sling. The other was some skinny nervous dude. He kept slapping his jeans pockets and eyeballing the door."

"Could you pick out these guys in a lineup?" Rick asked him. "Maybe recognize them from a mug shot?"

There's a high probability this will be a waste of time and effort, I thought. *We have no idea where these guys came from or how close the rock is that they crawled to and hid under.*

"I'll sure as hell try! Bring it on!"

A move to a much bigger room with more comfortable chairs, hundreds of photos and several glasses of water over two hours later, Duane used the pen to do more than scratch an itch.

"That's the guy from the bar with the busted arm." He drummed the tip of the pen on a photo and flipped a page in the spiral bound book of mug shots. "And that's nervous guy." Our witness had identified Troy Manning from Lethbridge, Alberta and Gary Duvall of Sudbury, Ontario. Each arrested for illegal possession of unlicensed handguns. Released six months ago after time served.

"You're sure about that?" I asked. "Sure enough to testify in court under oath?"

"You find them, Mountie, and I'll put my hand on that Bible and swear."

I promised Rick a six pack of beer and a home-cooked meal for his family as thanks for the best and only real lead we'd had. Colin drove us back to Ottawa.

"What's your take on all of this?" I asked my hand-picked and highly-recommended director of operations. Colin's record of commendations on exemplary investigative work both as RCMP and Canadian Security Intelligence Service surveillance officer nearly landed him my job and title.

"The two guys in the bar let rabble-rousing reinforcements in through the fire exit. That's why they needed that particular table."

Bang on, Colin. "That's what I thought, too. I meet with Commissioner Burke every Wednesday morning. I want you there with me tomorrow."

His nod acknowledged my request without taking his eyes off the road. "Then we better have a bullet point plan. The commissioner doesn't waste time or words."

"You're right about that. So we've got three hours of road time to look at what we've got and decide where we go with it."

Colin steered through the big city multi-lane bottleneck like a NASCAR pro. "Well, first we bring in Manning and Duvall. Find out if Lethbridge is the point of origin. If so, why, and if not then where exactly is."

"Agreed." I reached into the pocket of my uniform jacket for the leather-bound gold-initialed diary given to me by J-lynn on my thirty-fifth birthday. The first point penciled in jump-started our course of action to tear down a network of hate. "Then we connect the dots and tally up the numbers."

"Get a handle on how many rats are running and in what direction."

"Exactly."

Colin glanced in the driver's side mirror and flipped on the turn signal to safely pass a slower moving line of semis and a UPS delivery truck. "Has the bar brawl incidents count gone up?"

"Three confirmed since Toronto. Two more in Ontario. The first one reported in Quebec just last weekend."

"Where in Quebec?" Colin asked.

"Gatineau in Old Hull."

"That's too close for comfort. Same as in Toronto?"

"Similar. Mostly minor injuries. Major damage. Windows in the bar were broken out." That's when the warning bells went off in my head. I got on my cell phone and called the office.

"Grace, do me a favor. Get on the net and pull up the news report on the incident at the Gatineau bar last weekend. Yeah, that's it. Read it back to me." An employee on smoke break in the parking lot somehow got his hands on a fire extinguisher and saved the bar manager's car. A car on fire. Just and only like Victoria, Saskatoon and Toronto. "One more thing. I need to know the proximity of the bar from where the prime minister's mother lives. OK call me back. Thanks."

"A hunch?" Colin asked.

"More like a nagging fear." My cell phone lit up. "Yes, Grace."

"The bar is three blocks and around the corner from Celine Reid's residence," my assistant confirmed.

I ended the call and swore. *That's it. The last dot connected. The lines were in focus. The trail would end in my back yard.* "Disrupting the House of Commons vote is the distraction. The prime minister is the target."

Chapter 24

Jerilynn

The smile on Vincent Lockwood's moon face began to fade when I didn't leave the room.

"Vincent." The prime minister stood and circled the desk. His imposing height and handshake strength upped the obvious agenda setting advantage in his favor. "Good to see you. Please." My boss sat in one of a pair of identical straight backed leather chairs positioned in front of his desk. Lockwood settled his older and much wider body in the other. I sat on the sofa and cushion nearest my boss.

The back bencher frowned. "I was under the impression this would be a private meeting."

"My chief of staff has kept me apprised of your concerns regarding the amendment to Bill C-71. I asked her to sit in to ensure all the salient points are discussed." The prime minister leaned back in his chair. "Let's talk about those concerns."

Lockwood cleared his throat. "Well, the cost of the buyback and enforcement at the border ..."

"Are both valid concerns. The buyback is in the budget. Some municipalities, Toronto in particular, already have buyback programs for handguns as well as long guns. Enforcement at the border will increase once the amendment is approved by the Senate and goes to royal assent. But the fact is the majority of illegal guns in Canada are not smuggled across the border. They're bought or made here in Canada and resold on the black market for a considerable profit. It stands to reason making handguns illegal would be a legal deterrent. Would you agree, Vincent?"

Lockwood cleared his throat again. "That is a reasonable outcome for the sake of argument. But is it realistic?"

"That's a very good question. Here's another." The prime minister leaned forward and slightly toward me. "To achieve that reasonable outcome, our government must anticipate the argument, present the facts in debate and unify Liberal Party support for the amendment. The chair of the public safety committee can be most persuasive. I know Mr. Poirier persuaded you."

"But I wouldn't let him stall the amendment in committee. I made sure that amendment made it to second reading."

"I appreciate that. Now we all must do our part to convince a majority of MPs to positively consider an amendment that will help protect police officers and all Canadians from gun violence."

"My record of support for the party ..."

I interrupted him. "Mr. Lockwood, do you consider yourself a loyal member of the Liberal caucus?"

His mouth dropped open. For the first time in my memory, no sound came out. I took advantage of that rare event and asked another question. "Is the official opposition's objections to the amendment in line with yours?"

His cheeks flushed. He sputtered and wet his lips with his tongue. "I've been a loyal Liberal in Parliament for eighteen years!"

"I'm glad to hear that, Vincent," said the prime minister. "That answers Jerilynn's first question. What about the second?"

His fists clenched and unclenched with the blink of his eyes. "Poirier tried to kill the amendment by questioning the trustworthiness of this government because of the order-in-council from cabinet that banned assault weapons. He lied when he led me to believe that I was the only member of the committee he'd met with to discuss that concern."

"Anything else?" the prime minister asked.

"Well, I'm not sure if this is related to the amendment." Lock-wood swiped at the thin film of sweat on his forehead. "I went to his office to confront him when I found out he'd met with all the committee members. The door hadn't clicked closed. I was about to knock when I heard voices. Poirier was talking with someone. I could tell from the conversation that he wasn't from The Hill. Poirier said something about a money transfer for the cause."

"What cause?" I asked.

"I'm not sure. They didn't say. But it was a large sum. Over a million dollars. The man Poirier was meeting with said the money would be sent by noon the next day. I got out of there when the voices got closer to the door. That's all I know."

My boss and I kept our composure in the stunned silence that followed. "Should you overhear similar conversations or become aware of further details …"

"I will contact you immediately, Prime Minister."

"Thank you, Vincent. For now, I need to know. Can I count on your support for the handgun bill amendment?

"Yes. You have my support."

Following another round of handshakes and thank yous, I walked Lockwood out of the office. The prime minister was back behind his desk when I returned and closed the door.

"That was unexpected." *I dropped onto the couch. I've got nothing. What are you thinking, boss?*

"Power and the money to buy it are Poirier's weaknesses. He's broken campaign financing rules before. He might be going down that rat hole again." He sat back and stared out the window. "Is that what he's up to?"

I shivered at the prospect of another unthinkable possibility. Guns, money, politics and the lunatic fringe. My husband's words echoed in my head. I sincerely hoped I was wrong.

Chapter 25

Willie

The dreaded but necessary return to bed and sleep in the house he desperately wanted to leave but couldn't was interrupted by a text message from his sister.

Meet me at Timmy's when you get off work. Please! Urgent!

Heavy clouds in a pre-dawn sky opened and poured a chilly rain that soaked through Willie's pants and Maple Leafs jacket. He was too tired to run to his car. The hard splash in puddles would only make a bad situation worse.

The coffee shop parking lot was nearly full despite the long line of cars waiting to place orders in drive-through. Willie steered the sedan into one of the last open spots. Annabel waved to him from her seat at a table behind the window.

She stacked a pile of "For Rent" flyers on top of the creased and folded the newspaper to clear the table. "I was afraid you wouldn't get my message," she said. "Here." She set a large lidded take-away cup in front of him. "I got you a double-double."

"Thanks." Willie peeled the sleeves of the wet jacket from his arms and hung it on the back of the unoccupied chair next to him. "What's so urgent?"

"Fiona and I can't stay in that house anymore. I have got to find a place for us to live."

Willie sat down hard in the chair across from her. "What happened?"

Annabel circled long nails painted sunset red along the rim of her take-away lid. "Fiona didn't come home last night. She stayed at a friend's house. She called me this morning and said she won't come back. She'll run away if she has to. But she can't listen to her angry, alcoholic grandfather rage on and on about the liberals and Prince Privileged anymore."

"Did you say anything to Dad?" Willie cringed at the bitter bite in her laugh.

"Oh, yeah. He called her an ungrateful spoiled brat and told me I better get a second job because he's not gonna pay for her to go to that fancy private school in the fall." She dabbed a tear away from the corner of her eye. "Fuck him. We're moving out. I'll find someplace near the public school so she can walk. She doesn't like taking the bus anyway."

"Rent's not cheap."

"Don't you think I know that!" She fisted the flyers and slapped them on the newspaper. "I've only found a couple of options I can even come close to paying for." Willie's chest tightened at the plea in her voice mirrored in her eyes. "You could move out with us, Willie. With your paycheck maybe we'd have a chance to find a nice three bedroom apartment or a townhouse."

"What about Mom? We're all she lives for. And we'd be leaving her alone. With him."

Annabel sat back and slumped in the chair. "I know. But she won't leave. She stays in that hell to keep a wedding vow that he broke a long time ago. That bit about love, honor and cherish. What a load of crap."

I can't cut the last string Mom has to hang on to! "I don't want you and Fiona to go. I'll help you move out. I don't want to stay. I hate it there as much as you do." He got up and grabbed his coat. Residual rain dripped on his soggy shoes. "I'm sorry. But I can't come with you."

He shoved the untouched cup of coffee in the trash and walked out into the downpour.

Chapter 26

Alec

The secure email pings of progress began within an hour of Commissioner Burke's dispatched orders to RCMP Division Headquarters and detachments. The same message was forwarded to chiefs of police across all thirteen provinces and three territories.

"Identify and investigate reports of anti-government/pro-gun network cells and connections. Detain suspects for questioning. Arrest on suspicion of public incitement and willful promotion of hate speech Troy Manning and Gary Duvall. Photos of suspects and criminal record attached."

The report I wanted most came while J-lynn and I were feasting on Digby scallops.

"Yes, Commissioner." I wiped the butter and oil from the corners of my mouth with a cloth napkin.

"Ottawa PD has Manning and Duvall in custody."

"That was a quick collar."

"Apparently Mr. Manning ignores posted speed limits and fails to stop at red lights. I have requested that you and Operations Officer Landry be present when the suspects are questioned."

"When?"

"In twenty minutes."

"Thank you, Commissioner." I called Colin, told him when and where we needed to be on short notice, and forked the last of my meal into my mouth.

"What's up, love?" My wife's speared scallop hung on tines poised over her plate.

"Duty calls," I said and trotted upstairs to change back into my uniform.

She followed as I knew she would. "Does this have anything to do with the threat to the prime minister?"

"It does." I sat down on our bed, shoved my feet into spit-polished shoes, tugged on and tied the laces.

J-lynn stood in front of me, all five-foot-nothing of her, arms folded as if to block my impending exit. "Need I remind you of your promise to give me a heads up?"

"I remember and I will." Her pout was so cute and irresistible. My arms around her waist toppled her softly to the mattress. "Right now I've got to go." I kissed her quick, ran down the stairs and out the door to the marked RCMP vehicle I'd driven home.

A second vehicle with the same distinctive federal law enforcement markings parked in the space next to my cruiser exactly seventeen minutes later. Colin and I walked side-by-side into Ottawa PD HQ and down the hallway to a room with a window that only let us see who was on the other side. The uniformed officer at the door cranked up the volume control on the wall that allowed us to hear the questions and answers.

The belligerent man in hand cuffs shuffled in and kicked the chair the officer indicated he should sit in. Muscles bulged everywhere in a cross-fit trained body that appeared younger than the deep lines of age in his flushed red face. A man and woman dressed in plain clothes with badges clipped to their belts followed close behind. The door closed behind them.

"Mr. Manning," the female officer began and was quickly cut off.

"This is a free country and you have no right to hold me against my will!"

"Mr. Manning," the officer said again. "You and your associate Mr. Duvall are suspects in an ongoing investigation of criminal activity that has resulted in serious personal injuries and property damage."

Manning sneered and tried his best to spit at her. "You've got nothing on either of us."

"Well, yeah, we do." Her partner stepped to the opposite edge of the table from the chair Manning was in. "We have an eye witness that put you at the scene before and at the time when a fight broke out in a downtown Toronto bar. That same eye witness claims you and Mr. Duvall visited him in hospital and offered him money in exchange for not reporting your involvement to the authorities."

"That don't prove fuck all and you know it. Unless you've got another witness it's his word against ours." Manning leaned back in the chair. His smug smile revealed a single gold front tooth. "I know the law. You got twenty-four hours to either charge me or cut me loose. Either way I have the right to call an attorney." The smile disappeared. "When I do I'm gonna sue this piss poor police department, the city and the federal government because I am sure there's RCMPs on the other side of that mirror." He flipped us the middle finger salute.

"Well, he made his point. This is pointless," Colin said.

The plainclothes officers apparently agreed with us. The second suspect appeared minutes after Manning was led out. His hands in cuffs twitched. His line of sight never strayed far from the door.

"Nervous guy," I said.

"Yeah. This I like." Colin took off his jacket, loosened his tie and suggested that I do likewise. "We're going in." Colin motioned to the plainclothes officers at the open doorway to the interrogation room. "We've got this," he told them. He beckoned me to follow his lead and closed the door on the sputtering officers of the Ottawa PD.

"Good evening, Mr. Duvall." He smiled large and sat on the table with one foot on the floor. "I'm Officer Landry and this is Officer Martin. Can we get you anything? Glass of water? Soda?"

119

"I wanna talk to a lawyer."

"I'm sure you do. We're here to make sure you get everything you are entitled to. Coffee. Counsel. A reduced sentence." Colin leaned toward the smaller man with his chin now buried in his chest. Handcuffs hung as loose and limp as the size-too-big clothing covering his thin body. "We have an eyewitness that will testify your buddy Manning started a mini-war in a Toronto bar using hate speech and that, Mr. Duvall, is a felony. Especially when that hate speech causes bodily harm and threatens the safety of the prime minister and or a member of his staff."

"I have no idea what you're talking about."

"Well, then, let me refresh your memory. We have CCTV footage of you tampering with the vehicle owned by the prime minister's chief of staff."

The color in Duvall's cheeks faded to an even lighter shade of pale. "I don't believe you. You can't prove that!"

"Oh, yes we can. You see, we're not Ottawa PD. We're Parliamentary Protective Service. Are you at all familiar with what we are sworn to do?" Colin inched closer to Duval for emphasis. "Our jobs depend a great deal on keeping the prime minister and in fact everyone on Parliament Hill safe. And we will do anything to make sure he and they live a long and happy life. Am I making myself clear at all to you, Mr. Duvall?"

Duvall sniffed and wiped his nose on the sleeve of his denim shirt above his cuffed wrists. "You can't keep me here more than a day without proof that I broke the law."

Colin stood up and paced around the table, slow and deliberate, until he was within arm's length of the seated suspect. "You know what I did before I joined the RCMP? I was CSIS. Yeah. Before that I went to law school. Studied criminal law." Colin put his hand on the table for balance and emphasis. The look in his eyes transformed from sensible to satanic. "Don't waste your breath quoting the law to me. It's my Bible. I breathe it. I live it. Every day. What you're accused of is a matter of national security and a terrorist threat. If you're convicted, you won't see the light of day for the rest of your life."

After a respectable interval intended to foster fear, Colin straightened and retraced his paced steps. "However, if you agree to help us root out this threat, we will do everything we can to make your life much more comfortable and your time behind bars much, much less." When he turned back to Duvall, the large smile was back. "So. What do you say, Mr. Duvall. Can we count on your cooperation?"

When he spoke, Duvall's voice was as small as his presence in the room. "I don't know anything about a threat to the prime minister. The only contacts I know of are in Toronto and here."

"How many in Ottawa?" I asked.

"Three. Me. Manning. And another guy Manning knows but I don't. He gives the orders. We carry them out."

I went for broke and asked the most important question. "What are your orders for Wednesday the nineteenth?"

"We haven't gotten them yet. We're just supposed to show up and protest the anti-gun bill. Make a lot of noise. Carry signs and unloaded weapons." Nervous guy shut down. "I swear to you, that's all I know."

Colin opened the door to the hallway and signaled officers that our business with Duvall had concluded. "What's your take on this?" I asked him as Manning's accomplice was led away.

"Duvall may know more than he's telling us. Manning knows a lot more. That's the nut we have to crack."

"We're running out of time. Parliament debates the handgun ban bill amendment for the third and final time in six days. I got a feeling unknown caller is the guy giving the orders."

"Locking up two of his soldiers may slow him down. But it won't stop him."

"No, it won't," I said. "That's our job."

Chapter 27

Friday the 14th - Jerilynn

The prime minister signed and tapped his pen on the last of the papers from what had been a short stack of official documents. "That's it." He glanced at his wristwatch. "If I leave right now, I'll just make it to Corina's school play as promised. If I don't, I'll never hear the end of it."

The call that erased plans for a rare early start to a work free weekend came over a secure line. My boss frowned at the phone. "This can't be good," he said and picked up. "*Bonjour, Jean-Michel.*" His free hand signaled that I stay where I was with only the two of us behind a closed door. French President Jean-Michel Dumont had recently survived a neo-Fascist challenge to a second term in office by the skin of his political teeth. The prime minister and I had raised a glass of chardonnay at his Rideau Cottage office to toast our relief at the re-election of a left wing ally. "*Je veux que mon chef de cabinet entende cela.*" I want my chief of staff to hear this. "*Merci.*" The mid-volume conference call engaged with a click.

"Should I speak in English?"

"Whichever you prefer. Jerilynn is fluent."

"*Oui.* Of course she would be." The usual controlled cadence in his second language conveyed an unusual rush of tense urgency. "France needs Canada's help, Evan. Air France Flight 524 left Tel Aviv for Paris early this morning. The plane was commandeered an hour into the flight. The hijackers landed the plane in Algiers and allowed 74 passengers to deplane in exchange for fuel. Their original demand was to be allowed to land in New York City. The United States initially agreed. But as you know their government is much divided. Our request has since been refused. The president is under pressure from both his party and the opposition. They do not want to risk a repeat of the nine-eleven terrorist attack. I have spoken directly to what appears to be their leader and explained to him why the plane cannot land in the U.S. They have changed their demand and will land in another North American city."

"Which would be?"

"Toronto."

This can't be happening! Every muscle in my body seized up. I went cold as the last breath I'd taken froze.

The prime minister's jaw clenched. He swore under his breath through his teeth. "Too much risk. That's a long way into Canadian air space over too many potential targets."

"*Oui*. I understand and I agree."

"What is the size of the aircraft and how many people are on board?"

"The aircraft is a Boeing 777 with 316 passengers and crew, less the 74 elderly and mothers with children who deplaned in Algiers. I checked the passenger manifest. There are no Canadians on the flight."

"But there are 242 people still on board."

"And the hijackers. I could only distinguish four separate voices in the cockpit - the pilot, the co-pilot and two other men."

Breathe! Move! My right hand pushed the pen in it. Scribbled notes appeared on the page. The fingers on my left tapped and sent urgent reply text messages into the cell phone.

"How the hell did they get into the cockpit?"

"I am not sure. But they must have had accomplices on the plane to make that possible, more than likely among the crew."

"Do we know who these people are? What they want?"

"As I've said, I have spoken directly with one of the men in the cockpit. All he would say was that his people want to take the message of their suffering and oppression directly to their oppressors."

"No mention of a specific terrorist group?"

"*Non*." The French president paused to listen and reply to someone in the room with him. "The clock is ticking, Evan. I am in desperate need of an answer."

"Let me confer with my chief of staff."

"Of course."

"Jerilynn, alert .."

"The deputy prime minister, the governor general, ministers of national defence, foreign affairs, public safety and emergency preparedness, the attorney general and General VanDuyne. Done. What about the opposition leaders?"

He hesitated for a moment. "Oh, sure, why not. God forbid I should be accused of exclusion."

The replies streamed in. The governor general was on her way back to Ottawa from Vancouver as was the leader of the NDP. The attorney general was at home in her Calgary riding office but would return if requested. "Just say the word, Prime Minister," Hannah Jeffries responded. My boss thanked and briefed her over the phone. During the anxious minutes of uncounted hours, National Defence Minister Dominic Fornier, Chief of Defence Staff General Forrest VanDuyne, Deputy Prime Minister Carla Mendez, Foreign Affairs Minister Alicia Singh and David Getti, minister of public safety and emergency preparedness arrived and gathered around the prime minister's desk.

Minister Fornier was the first to say the only possible option from the discussion. "For the sake of national security, the plane must land at Gander."

"Agreed," General VanDuyne said as Conservative Party Leader Richard Lowe and Marc Tremblay, leader of the Bloc Quebecois, strode in and joined the circle.

"What has been agreed?" Lowe sat in the unoccupied chair closest to the prime minister, ankle crossed over his knee.

"Gander is the only acceptable destination for the hijacked Air France flight." The prime minister reached for the phone and line that would reconnect him with Paris. The minister of defence ordered General VanDuyne to mobilize 9 Wing Gander and 5 Wing Goose Bay out of Labrador.

"Wait a minute!" Lowe got to his feet. "Are we going to let an aircraft with potentially hostile radicals touch down on Canadian soil?"

"We must!" Tremblay weighed in. "The President of France has asked for our help. Do you want the stain of the innocents' blood on our hands?"

"Gentlemen, this is not a debate. You are here as a courtesy of protocol." The prime minister called President Dumont. "Jean-Michel, Canada will allow Flight 524 to land at Gander International Airport in Newfoundland."

"Merci. I will inform the pilot. But I expect the hijackers will not be pleased."

"Gander and Goose Bay are ready and airborne," General VanDuyne reported. "NORAD confirms Flight 524 will enter Canadian air space in forty minutes. The current flight plan heading takes the plane to Pearson."

"Pearson!" Lowe planted his palms on the prime minister's desk and leaned as far forward as possible. "That's Toronto!"

"I'm well aware of that." The dangerous outward sign of anger darkened my boss' eyes.

"Evan, the hijackers are resisting. I can patch this line directly through to the cockpit," President Dumont said.

"Go ahead." The prime minister covered the phone's mouthpiece with his palm. "Dominic, advise the governor general."

"Yes, Prime Minister." Minister Fornier turned to his chief of defence staff. "General, order the RCAF at Gander to escort the plane from sighting to ground. Scramble and intercept."

"Yes, sir."

"What does that mean?" Tremblay asked.

"It means if the plane doesn't go where we want it to go, the prime minister can order it shot down," the deputy prime minister told him.

"That is inhumane!" Tremblay shouted.

"So what would you suggest?" The minister of public safety shot back. "Let a hijacked plane fly twenty seven hundred kilometers into Canadian air space to our most densely populated city?"

"Who am I speaking to?" The thick tongue accent from an unidentified Middle Eastern region of the world spoke through desk phone conference call.

"You are speaking to Evan Reid, the Prime Minister of Canada. Identify yourself."

"That is of no concern."

"It is to me."

"My soldiers and I are in control of this plane. We will land in Toronto."

"I have cleared Flight 524 to land at Gander International Airport in Newfoundland."

"That is not an acceptable destination."

"It is the only point of entry available to you in Canada. Check the radar. Those are CF-18 fighter jets. The Royal Canadian Air Force has been ordered to escort Flight 524 to Gander."

No one spoke or moved during the long nerve-fraying pause for response. "We will only land in Toronto."

The prime minister's eyes narrowed. "If that plane is not headed for Gander International Airport, the minute it crosses into Canadian air space, I will give the order and blow you to hell."

The collective gasp and nervous shift in chairs rose as one reactive sound and faded to silence.

"You are bluffing." The hijacker's voice faltered.

The prime minister's did not. "When the safety of my people is on the line, I don't bluff."

Everyone shifted their full attention to General VanDuyne when he entered the PM's office at the culmination of more tense moments. "Air traffic control reports Flight 524 is headed to Gander under CF-18 escort."

Waves of released relief circled the room in various forms of verbal expression.

"Well played, Prime Minister," said Minister Singh.

That was the wrong response.

My boss glared at his minister of foreign affairs. "This was not a game." Smoldering residual heat clung to his words.

The minister's shoulders dipped in deference. "Of course not. My apologies."

The prime minister took a deep breath and leaned back in his chair. "Thank you, everyone.

The room eventually cleared. I stayed, seated in the chair I'd been in when this life-and-death drama began.

"This time the string didn't break." I barely heard the words he spoke.

"Pardon me?"

"I hold a string that's connected to every person in this country, every country in the world. It's only one string of many. But if I pull it too hard and it breaks, the chain reaction I start could be catastrophic." He stared out the tall window panes streaked with rain and clouded by the grey gloom of a fading day. The demands of the job had darkened the shadows under his eyes and aged him years in a matter of hours. "Go home. Enjoy your weekend."

"Yes, Prime Minister. You as well."

You certainly earned it. I dodged heavy raindrops on my way to the parking lot and summoned his detail to take him home.

Chapter 28

Evan

Images of what could have gone wrong hung like ragged bits of peeling wallpaper behind the burn in my eyes.

"Have a good evening, Prime Minister." The protective detail's transport vehicle rolled to a stop at Rideau Cottage. I got out of the opened rear car door, thanked the plainclothes RCMP officers that had seen me safely home, and wondered why the security around me was at a higher state of readiness. For and against what, I couldn't be sure.

The trudge up the pathway and steps to and through the front door felt like a ten kilometer run. The family heirloom clock we'd brought with us when we moved in almost eight years ago chimed nine times from its position of honour on the mantel over the fireplace. I rejected the idea of checking whatever might await attention in my office down the hall and instead wandered toward the beam of overhead light from the kitchen.

Angeline sat at the table with her back to the door. Her idle hands clasped a cup of something that didn't look drinkable. She stared out the window into the darkness and didn't seem to notice me standing beside her.

She moved away from the caress of my fingers on her neck along the collar of her robe. "What's wrong, sweetheart?" I asked although I had a pretty good idea of what her answer would be.

"Everything is wrong." The sky blue eyes that always reminded me of a warm summer day had turned cold from a brewing inner storm.

"Look, I'm sorry I couldn't make it to Corina's play. I was all set to leave early until the phone call ..."

"I really don't want to hear the latest excuse." Her gaze turned away from me and back to the window. "While we're on the topic of phone calls, have you been ignoring the Liberal Party as well as your family?"

I sat down to keep from falling over. "What's that supposed to mean?"

"The phone was ringing when we came home from the school. The question wasn't asked directly. But I'm guessing that your party thinks that I am the reason you have not given them an answer." She got up from the table with the cup still in her hands and tossed the congealed contents down the sink. "I think they may be right."

I stayed where I was. "Right about what exactly?"

"I want you to tell them no." Her controlled flat tone frightened me. "Tell them eight years is enough because it's certainly enough for me."

Soft slipper footsteps fell in paced circles behind me. I listened without comment as my wife released pent up anger and frustration in a low voice so as not to disturb our children.

"Do you have any idea how many birthday parties and parent teacher conferences and dance recitals and hockey games and school plays and God only knows what else you've missed? I've lost count. I'm tired of being a single parent. I'm tired of making excuses for you and wiping away tears and promising ice cream to make up for the disappointment of Daddy not being there again. I can't do it anymore! It's not fair to our children, to me or to you!"

The pacing stopped. "Why should we have to sacrifice our lives while you play nanny to Parliament and the premiers? Someone else in the party needs to step up." She sat down hard in the chair she'd been in. "What are you going to tell them? Talk to me, Evan!"

I couldn't look at her. I was afraid of what I might see. "What do you want me to say? I know the party needs an answer and I haven't got one yet."

"Well I do." She took my hands in hers and held them to her lips. "I love you. I've stood by you and been here for you every step of the way." The most beautiful woman I would ever know, the other half of myself I could never live without took her hands away from mine. "But I swear if you tell them yes, our marriage is over. I will take the children and I will leave you."

When she stood and walked away she had with her pieces of the heart that she'd ripped out of me. I climbed the stairs hoping to get those pieces back. What happened next shattered what little was left.

"Daddy?" The tiny voice of my littlest angel called out from behind the half closed door to her bedroom. My hand on the door opened it wider. "Hey, pretty girl."

"C'mere." Her arms reaching out to me cast shadows in the dim night light she needed to feel safe enough to sleep. I walked to her, sat on the bed beside her, and held her in my arms. "You missed my play."

"I know and I'm sorry." I brushed the knot of curls from her forehead. "So, tell me about your play."

"You have to guess what I was."

"Were you a pirate?"

"No."

"A puppy dog?"

"No."

"A butterfly?"

"No. But I did have wings."

"You were a bird!"

"Daddy! I was a fairy princess."

"Oh, I see. What color were your wings?"

"A fairy princess always has pink wings. Everybody knows that."

"Is that so?" I hugged her close and buried my nose in the thick tufts of her hair. So like mine and my mother's but with the fragrant scent of a child I hardly knew. Could the baby I'd rocked to sleep really be seven years old? Angeline was right. I'd missed so much that I would never get back.

"Daddy. Gabby's birthday is next week. We're gonna have a party with thirteen candles on the cake. Gramma will be here. Mommy says there's gonna be a sleepover and it'll be so much fun."

Gabby. Gabrielle. Our firstborn a teenager. I counted off the dates in my head. Wednesday the nineteenth. The day of third reading for the handgun ban bill amendment in Parliament.

"Will you be at the party, Daddy?"

I closed my eyes tight to fight back tears I could not bear to let her see.

"I'll try, pretty girl."

The soft pat of her hand on my chest, her kiss on my cheek, and the plea she made tore my insides apart.

"Try real hard, Daddy," she said.

"I will, *mon petit ange.*" I held her until she slept peaceful, safe and oh so loved. Being careful not to wake her or anyone else, I went back downstairs, sat in the room where my Angeline, our children and I had strung garland and hung ornaments on Christmas trees, and wept.

Sleep would not be an option for me tonight.

Chapter 28

Saturday the 15th – Willie

The nightmare that woke Willie ended with a spark, a puff of smoke, a loud bang and a scream. Only the scream was real.

He scooped up his robe from the floor of the bedroom and ran down the stairs in stocking feet. His sister knelt at the bottom hunched over the shattered remains of a music box Willie had given her the Christmas after Fiona was born. When the lid with the grinning brown cow, a calico cat and a crescent moon was lifted the music played as long as the winding stem underneath turned. Hey diddle, diddle the cat and the fiddle the cow jumped over the moon would serenade Annabel no more.

She wept over the jagged pieces and shards of porcelain. "That was mine, you bastard!" Annabel screamed at their father.

Willie reached him in time to stop the swing of his arm and the open hand aimed at his sister's face. "Don't you dare call me that!" William jerked away from his son. "Let go of me!" The smell of alcohol on his breath hung in the air with the bitter heat of his hate. He stumbled backward and fell against the kitchen table. His flat palms on its top steadied him but the jolt toppled a half-full plastic pitcher of orange juice. Willie's mom shuffled in from her sanctuary on the sun porch. Top of the hour. Eight a.m. CBC News radio reported the latest from Parliament Hill.

"Leave it!" William shouted at his frightened wife. "And turn that damn radio off! I have no interest in hearing the latest edict from Prince Privileged!" He re-directed his wrath at his daughter cradling the remnants of a cherished gift and memories. "Where's YOUR bastard? Huh? Haven't seen her in days!"

"That's because she's already moved out! I'm going with her. Today!"

"Good riddance! Ungrateful spoiled brats. Both of you!" William shouted and turned to his son. "Then there's YOU! I've put a roof over your head. Got you a job. Tried my damnedest to do everything I could to make you worth a damn. And look at you!" He invaded Willie's space, his nose inches from his son's. "Thirty five years old and still living at home with Mom and Dad."

"This has never been a home," Willie said. "I've stayed here because I had to."

"You stayed because you're a loser!"

"That's rich coming from you! The voters in your riding kicked you out of Parliament and then wouldn't let you back in!"

Willie tasted the blood before he felt the pain. His world tilted sideways. A second scream from his sister echoed in the advancing emptiness behind his eyes. He fought back, regained his senses, and threw a fisted punch at the object in the blur of his peripheral vision. The squish of soft tissue under his knuckles and the audible "oof" told Willie he'd hit his mark.

"Stop it!" Willie heard his mother screech, saw her palms pressed against her cheeks in horror at what she'd witnessed, like a painting he'd seen at an exhibition. He spit blood and worked his jaw. It still opened and closed. But it hurt. Bad.

"Willie! Oh, my sweet boy!" He winced when his mother pressed the cold water-soaked kitchen towel against the open cut. The raised edge Masonic insignia on the ring his father wore had branded the flesh below Willie's cheekbone.

William wheezed and lifted himself into a kitchen chair. "What about me?" he grunted.

"Fuck you!" Annabel grabbed flattened empty boxes from the short stack on the front room floor and ran up the stairs.

The images from Willie's waking dream appeared in surreal detail. His father's half-open, unseeing eyes. The silent scream. The blood Willie knew he could not spill. I wish it was real. I wish you were dead. "What she said." Willie sat on a step and lowered his head to battle the spin. A drop of blood from a loose tooth passed through his open lips.

Rose turned on her husband. "You should be ashamed of yourself," she scolded. "What kind of man raises his hand to his daughter and hits his own son?" She smoothed back Willie's poker straight brown hair and studied his injury. "I'll go get some ointment and a bandage." The slippers on her feet slapped the hardwood floor toward the main floor bath.

"William." His father coughed and rubbed his belly. "I'm …"

"Sorry?" Willie looked up and over the swelling below his left eye. "No, you're not. You've never been sorry about anything in your entire miserable life. Except losing two elections." He stood, turned, and used the banister for balance and a hand-over-hand hoist to ascend the stairs.

"Where are you going, Willie?" his mother called up after him.

"Anywhere else." He leaned against the upstairs wall between bedrooms. His sister was packing what was hers and Fiona's into unfolded boxes. He helped her assemble the lids.

"I am not staying in this house another minute! Are you sure you won't come with us? We can get a rollaway bed or a fold out couch."

"I'm going to call Henry. See if I can stay with him for the weekend."

"Then what?"

"I haven't made up my mind yet."

136

She dragged a full suitcase from Fiona's empty bed to the hallway. A glance at the injuries their father had inflicted on her brother momentarily stopped her frantic forward momentum. "You better get some ice on that bruise." Annabel kissed Willie's other cheek. "You'll always be welcome with us. You know that, don't you?"

"Yeah, I do. Thanks." They hugged and held on to each other as they'd done since childhood. Sibling soldiers on a domestic battle-ground.

"Take care of yourself, Willie."

"Take care of you and Fiona."

He let her go to move on. Willie dug out his cell phone from the pocket of the Maple Leafs jacket he'd tossed on his bed and called the only friend he had.

Chapter 29

Willie and Henry

The smile on Henry's face when he opened his front door turned down with an uttered curse. "Bloody hell, man!" He reached out for Willie's arm, helped him settle on the U-shaped sectional surrounding the wide-screen TV mounted on the wall, and closed the door on the outside world. "What happened? You look like you got in a fight and the other guy won."

"Nobody won. I think we both lost the day I was born." Willie held his pain in his palms. His jaw throbbed. His left eye had swollen to a slit that allowed only a sliver of light and blurred movement through to his brain. "The old man doesn't like being reminded of that."

Henry left the room and came back with an ice bag. He handed it to Willie and sat down next to him a cushion-width away. "Are you telling me your father did this to you?"

"The one and only."

"What a bastard."

"Yeah, that's what my sister called him, too. I did land a punch that knocked the wind out of him. He tried to apologize. I wouldn't let him."

"Was anyone else at home?"

"Just my Mom. My niece Fiona has already moved out. My sister is moving out as we speak. I think that's why the old man was so pissed off. It didn't help that he was already half-assed drunk."

"Is this why you wanted me to show you how to handle a gun? So that you could defend yourself and the women if you had to?"

Willie didn't have an answer. He'd dismissed the intent he'd had. Twice.

Henry interpreted his hesitant silence as a yes. "Aw, Willie." Henry got up and paced the big oval brown and gold braided rug on the floor between the sectional and the TV. "You couldn't point a gun at your own flesh and blood and pull the trigger. You're not that kind of guy." Henry paced a straight line to his front room window. The boys next door were engaged in a lively game of street hockey with their neighborhood rivals. An amateur pickup preview of hockey night in Canada. A slapped puck sailed over the makeshift goal posts and crossbar. He almost pumped his arms and joined in with their hiss of victory. Henry turned back to Willie. "It's up to you. But if it were me, I'd go to hospital get checked over then file a report with the police."

"No, I'm not gonna do that. He's a lawyer. I don't know how or if that could mess with his practice and license. Besides, he'd fight it. My Mom and Annabel would have to testify or at least make a statement." Willie shifted the ice bag from his eye to his jaw. "I'm not gonna put them through that."

Henry noticed the dried blood around the corner of Willie's mouth. "Will you be able to eat anything?"

Willie tested his jaw again. The loose tooth shifted with the touch of his tongue. "I guess. Probably wouldn't be able to chew steak or anything like that, though."

"How about I fry up some chicken? Maybe mash some potatoes? We'll wash it down with beers in front of this one-eyed monster. Watch the Leafs snatch defeat from the jaws of victory another Saturday night."

"I'd like that." Willie looked down at the ice bag in his hands. "I was gonna ask you if I could stay here tonight and tomorrow until I have to go to work Sunday night."

"You sure can, buddy. Did you bring a change of clothes? Your uniform?"

Willie nodded. "Yeah. It's in the car."

Henry extended his hand palm up. "Give me the keys. I'll go get your stuff."

"Thanks." Willie took off his jacket and handed over the keys from its pocket.

"I still think you should file a report. But that's your business."

Willie heard his friend call out to someone outside his front door as he went through and closed it. Heard younger voices shout back and wondered what it would have been like to grow up happy. He thought about what Henry had said. He was right.

I can't kill him. I can't even turn him in. I've got to do something. What can I do to sober him up and shut him up?

The weight of the gun in his mind was in his hand. The flash. The smell. The body jerking, convulsing, folding, falling. Blood staining the floor. The dead half-open eyes.

Willie couldn't harm anyone he knew well enough to call by name. But he could kill a stranger.

Chapter 30

Sunday the 16th ~ Alec

The land line ring on the dresser near my ear woke me too early on Sunday morning. I tossed back the covers as carefully as I could so as not to wake the sleeping beauty at my side. With the phone in one hand and my robe in the other, I hurried down the hallway and stairs.

"Alec Martin." I covered my half-naked self in a slight-of-hand and arm maneuver through the sleeves of the robe.

"Sir, an unmarked white van has been parked in the visitor's lot since Friday afternoon. No names on any of the sign in lists. Ontario plates. The registered owner is deceased."

"Have you called Ottawa PD?"

"Yes, sir. Officers and the bomb squad are here. They've dispatched a tow truck."

I could have just let them handle it and gone back to bed. But I didn't. I couldn't. "Don't tow it. I'm on my way." I dressed as quickly and quietly as possible, wrote a note for J-lynn, and drove through the first partly cloudy rose-to-gold stripes of dawn.

Ottawa PD had arrived with a canine unit trained to sniff out whatever shouldn't be there. "Find anything?" I asked the uniformed officer at the other end of the leash.

"Nothing. We've checked for wires that could trigger explosives. The van wasn't locked."

Both driver and passenger side doors were open. I walked around to the back of the vehicle. Duel doors opened to what appeared to be an empty interior. I hoisted myself up and in. My gloved hands along the inside walls and floor touched every inch of metal. *What's this custom option?* Compartments had been installed over the wheel wells. Metal rings lay flush on floor panels. I lifted the lids. The hinges made no sound.

141

I crawled out the way I came in and slammed the front doors closed. "Was the dog inside the van?"

"No. It was empty so I didn't see any need to."

I led dog and officer around to the open back doors. The dog jumped in and within seconds reacted to the scent.

"Guns."

"Are you sure?" I asked. "Not drugs or some other contraband?"

"He's been trained to sense firearms. We've been together seven years. I know his signals. He smells guns."

"Don't let anyone else in this van. Get forensics here to dust for prints." The cell phone in my pants pocket buzzed. J-lynn. But hers was not the name displayed.

"I so enjoy watching losers chase their tails."

"This game is getting old, don't you think? Let's play it out in the open. Where are you?"

"I'm close and getting closer."

I turned a full three-sixty and spotted a jogger wearing electric blue sweats. A thirty-something couple walking a standard poodle. A teen-aged boy skimming the sidewalk on a skateboard. Nothing out of the Sunday morning ordinary. "What do you want? Tell me who you are."

"I want revenge for a lie, Smart Alec." The call from unknown caller ended.

"Dammit!" I thumbed through my contacts. Rick picked up.

"Whatcha got, Smart Alec?"

"Funny you should ask. Who else at the academy called me that?"

142

"Smart Alec? Most of the cadets. A couple of our instructors. You were a competitive pain in more than a few butts. Why?"

"There was a cadet in our class that got kicked out."

"Yeah, I remember. A real bad apple. Always pissed off. Punched a guy during role play and broke his nose. Argued investigative procedure with the facilitators. You called him out for taking a gun without permission."

"I double checked the inventory. A sidearm went missing and I reported it. He was the last guy I saw near the weapons. What the fuck was his name?"

"Joe or Jay or Jim something."

The flicker of memory flared with Rick's cued clue.

"James Mobley."

"You think he's involved in all this?"

"That's the best working theory I've got."

"Let me know when you've got more."

The call ended with a promise to keep Rick apprised. I paced the scene and stressed the high priority need for even a partial print with every investigating Ottawa officer on site. My wife called as the van was towed away.

"Sorry, I couldn't wait any longer. I got worried. What's going on?"

"I'm not sure yet."

"Great. That's just what I need. Another mystery."

"I'll tell you mine if you tell me yours."

"Why do I always have to go first?"

"Corroborative evidence."

"Whatever, Alec. The prime minister just called. He's taking a personal day tomorrow."

"And that's significant because?"

"Usually it wouldn't be. But there's a lot of work to be done before Wednesday. I guess that will just make for a very long and exhausting Tuesday. I might go back to bed after I scrub his Monday itinerary from the government website."

"Where is the PM supposed to be tomorrow?"

"His schedule off The Hill is light. Just a two o'clock at his constituency office in Vanier. A thank you to the long haul loyal staff and volunteers and a pep talk ahead of the election campaign."

That's where he'll make his move. That's how we'll smoke him out! I'd driven past the flat roof building that housed a handful of storefront offices almost every day on my way to or from work. The never-ending construction zone around it would be a surveillance challenge. But there were only so many places where a sharpshooter could hide. "Don't cancel it! I'll explain later. Thanks, love. I've gotta go."

"Hey! When are you …" I knew cutting her off would cost me. But my need to act fast was greater than her need to know.

I called the commissioner to report details she likely knew and a plan that she didn't. "I don't have anything that ties Mobley to this investigation. All I've got is based on conjecture and circumstantial evidence."

"What you're asking me to approve will be very difficult to explain and defend if the time and resources required are wasted. However, the risk is worth the potential reward. Go ahead, Chief."

"Thank you, Commissioner."

I called Colin along the walk to my office. We had a lot of work to do and only a day to do it.

Chapter 31

Willie

Global News was reporting the latest violent confrontation in the Middle East when Willie woke from his nap. He swung his legs over the side of the sectional's cushions and forced himself to sit up. Time marked on the clock mounted to the left of the big screen TV on Henry's front room wall gave him ninety minutes to change into his uniform and report for the night security shift on Parliament Hill.

The recliner with Henry in it was stretched out and back as far as it would go. Three empty bottles of beer littered the floor around it. Another had slipped from Henry's hand and lodged between the armrest and his hip. Soft snores accompanied by the occasional bubble of saliva from partially opened lips confirmed his friend's deep state of slumber.

Willie inspected the wound and bruise on his cheek in the bathroom mirror. At least his eye was open. He washed up, changed into his uniform, and gathered up what he had brought with him. His weekend respite had given him time to think.

It's now or never.

Willie had a plan.

Henry kept his handgun on the top shelf in the closet of his bedroom. Willie had watched him put it away. He'd memorized the combinations of the locks that secured the case and the trigger cable. He stood in the hall between the doorways to the bath and the master bedroom in the five room bungalow.

Stop! Listen!

Henry was still snoring.

Willie's sock covered feet made no sound on the carpet that covered the floor. He took care to open drawers slowly. Underwear, socks and junk items scattered from his hands to the bed and the top of the dresser. Arms of shirts that had been in the closet hung limp over the sides of the bed. Shuffled shoes piled on false evidence of an intruder's search for valuables. He lifted the gun case from the shelf and gripped the handle.

I'm not stealing. He'll get it back.

Straps attached to his bag of belongings slung over his shoulder. He made his way back down the hallway to the back door. Take it slow! The bolt in the lock eased open with the careful turn of his wrist.

The deck of cards from Henry's last game of solitaire lay in half play display on the kitchen table.

I'll take this one.

Willie pocketed the jack of clubs in his Maple Leafs jacket.

He stepped past the spot where he'd slept last night and napped the late afternoon into evening. Global News programming had changed to broadcast infotainment. Willie locked the front door on his way out.

Henry had slept through it all.

A blanket in the back seat of Willie's car covered the gun case. Light traffic along well lit streets and synchronized stop lights allowed him ample time to park in a spot near the door partially obscured by equipment and materials for Centre Block renovations. Willie knew where the cameras were. Knew where he could and would not be seen.

This is it.

He got out of his car, covered the gun case with his jacket and slid the jack of clubs in the door frame sweet spot. The light turned green. He opened the door and closed it quickly. The alarm didn't sound.

I'm in!

Guards working the shift before his were out in the halls and away from the locker room. Willie shielded the gun case with his jacket and stashed the secured weapon inside and behind a locked metal door. He reversed his course back to the hidden door and used the card once more. The lock clicked closed. He breathed in the cool night air on the edge of construction and squelched the urge to laugh out loud at his success.

Effortless entry gained him building access the usual way. A wave of greeting and good nights exchanged ended the second shift. Willie poured and drank his first cup of coffee, checked the employee message board, and began his nightly rounds.

Chapter 32

Monday the 17ᵗʰ - Alec

Tired clichés crossed my mind in the exhaustive lead up to set a trap. Burning the midnight oil. Battle lines being drawn. Boots on the ground. Others I'd rather forget.

Ottawa PD went on alert with the call from Chris Burke. Around midnight, forensics confirmed the possible and likely identity of our suspect. All of the fingerprints on the van belonged to law enforcement personnel except one. A partial print on the driver's seat adjustment lever matched a dishonourably discharged RCMP cadet and the federal criminal record of James Mobley, arrested three years ago along with Troy Manning for unauthorized possession of a handgun. Manning's sentence was suspended. Mobley served the maximum six months in prison.

I checked in with J-lynn as soon and as often as I could. Her heightened level of annoyance immediately pivoted professional with the reality of police action bullet points.

"Sherry Jackson is your contact at the constituency office. I filled her in. She's aware the prime minister will not be there but preparations for his expected visit will go forward."

"What about the media?" I asked.

"A low key news release was sent out last week. Not much response or interest. My sense is they're holding out for the big event on Wednesday."

"Good. Let's keep it that way."

"Alec." Her tone shifted protective. "Be careful. This guy Mobley has it in for you. When he sees my boss isn't there, that he's been duped, he'll take it out on you."

"Don't worry. I'll be ready."

I could hear the fear in her pause. "Promise you'll be home for dinner tomorrow night."

The tremor in her voice tumbled me back in time to the little boy in navy blue pajamas and thick red wool socks with a one-eyed teddy bear tucked under his arm. The voice was my mother's. The larger-than-life man in the Mountie uniform and spit-shined boots was my dad.

"I promise." I answered my wife as he had and said a silent prayer to make it so.

Chapter 33

The Big Man

The rear tire drop into a pothole rattled the frame of the older model van pockmarked with dents large and small. Hands the size of dinner plates gripped the steering wheel. The rebound bounce to concrete sloshed cold coffee over the open rim of the takeout cup in the holder next to the driver's knee. "Damned old rust bucket." James Mobley cursed the worn out shocks and broken spring cause for the sudden dampness on his jeans.

The white van in police lockup had transported hundreds of illegal assault weapons, handguns and thousands of rounds of ammunition to network cells in six provinces. *Watching Smart Alec sniff around like a canine unit on the commissioner's leash was worth having to abandon that ride on Parliament Hill.* He laughed out loud to no one.

Beams from dim headlights lit the brick exterior of the guest house. The van bounced and lurched to a stop. Mobley grabbed a bag from the passenger seat and climbed the stairs to the second floor. He'd left the lights on in the hallway and suite.

Mobley opened the mini-fridge and the last can of beer. He dumped the contents of the bag onto the bed he'd slept in every night for the last six weeks. The stained brown bib overalls, scuffed steel toe work boots and generic yellow hard hat he'd scored in a second hand store would get him in. No questions asked. The plan in his head was flawless. Textbook role play scenario from the RCMP cadet training manuals. He'd drive that sorry excuse for a vehicle to the parking garage construction site. Mobley had observed the ebb and flow of the workers. Waited until their workday ended. Staked out the most secluded spot on the second level with the best angle and view of the curb and sidewalk across the street.

He lifted the lid on the toolbox he would carry under his arm. The deconstructed M14 rifle still in his possession fit there like it belonged. Mobley had practiced for hours. He'd trained himself to assemble and load the rifle in three minutes flat. He'd get in position. Take the shot. Leave the weapon. Walk away empty handed. Hail a cab to the airport and fly to New Brunswick. Pick up another new van in St. John loaded with guns and ammo for delivery to Atlantic Canada. He'd personally recruit network members in Nova Scotia. Mobley would get perverse pleasure at flaunting his success in Alec's home province.

The TV remote lay next to the hard hat on the bed. The screen flickered on at Mobley's touch. Broadcast news reported the lead up to Wednesday's House of Commons debate and vote on the handgun ban amendment. Mobley snorted as images briefly flashed with captions and no volume. The House of Commons. Evan Reid. Alec Martin's lip service assurance of increased security on Parliament Hill. The prime minister's Monday PR appearance in Vanier rated a less than thirty second talking head mention.

"Here's to tomorrow." He lifted the can in mock salute and gulped the beer.

Chapter 34

Alec

The caffeine buzz in my sleep-deprived brain amplified the piercing squawk through the earpiece. I blinked and willed the pain behind my eyes to subside. In paired formation we waited. RCMP alongside Ottawa PD. No uniforms. All of us dressed in civilian daily ordinary from business suits to jeans and sweats.

"In position LCBO." Customers hustled in and out of the liquor store on the opposite street corner.

"Ready on the rooftop." Our best shooters with scopes on rifles crouched behind a three-foot concrete block wall around the edge of the flat roof over our heads.

"Parking garage report." Colin's voice came from behind and through my earpiece.

"In position. No unusual activity."

"Something's missing." I scanned the pedestrian and vehicle traffic through the windows of the vacant storefront next door to the Vanier Liberal Party constituency office.

"Yeah, there is. The rat."

"I'll rephrase. What am I missing?"

Colin glanced at his wristwatch. "Whatever it is, we've only got a half hour to figure it out."

I backed away from the window and stared out at the street. My gaze traced the steel and concrete outline of the triple deck parking garage under construction directly across the street. *Where would I go if I were Mobley? Where would I be to take the shot? I paced the empty space between the walls. How would I walk away?*

A role play exercise I'd botched as a cadet resurfaced in embarrassing detail. I'd followed procedure by the book. Looked for and expected the obvious. That strategy had defeated me. I'd been disarmed. The sniper's intended 'victim' died. "Something about this scenario seems too familiar." *Had Mobley been kicked out of the academy before or after I made that mock fatal error?* "Parking garage."

"Go ahead."

"Ask the foreman if there are any workers or vehicles on site for the first time today." I didn't wait for an answer. "I'm going to check out the construction site."

Colin raised an eyebrow. "To look for what you're missing?"

"Exactly." I used the rear exit, crossed the street and circled around back of the eventual three level car park. Covered street level and second floors were complete. The unfinished top floor was open to a darkly overcast sky threatening rain.

Officers stood at either end of the standard sidewalk width span of space between the LCBO and the garage. I recognized the man talking with the officer nearest the rear access driveway and temporary parking lot. The site foreman wore the layer of dust on his clothes like a uniform.

"Chief Superintendent Martin, right?" He removed his hard hat and wiped sweat and dust from his forehead with a shop rag pulled from his pocket. "One of our contractors sent a new guy over this morning. That's his truck." He pointed to a pale yellow van that had obviously seen better days. "Big dude. Didn't say much. Just handed over his paperwork."

"The papers were legit?"

He shrugged. "I guess so. Truth be told, I didn't look real close."

"Did he have anything with him?"

"Metal tool box under his arm. Hinged lid. Handles on the ends."

"Is he working on the top level?" I asked.

"Not likely."

"Why not?"

"Short term workers aren't allowed up there. Stairs aren't finished. The shafts have been installed. But the elevators aren't working yet. The only way to get to the top is by cherry picker."

"So the regular crews are working on the third level?"

"That's right. The short term contractors are on main floor finish work. They'll move up to second floor by the end of the week."

That's where that fucker Mobley is. That's where he'll take the shot. "Mind if I have a look around?"

"No problem." He handed over the hard hat. "Take this. Put it on. I'm going on break."

I stepped through and around the maze of pails, piles of metal and tools of the trade used by workers on their way off site with thermoses and uncapped water bottles. Bright overhead lights cast no shadows on the cement block cave stairwell.

Don't give away your position. I forced myself to breathe. *Steady. Slow. Make no sound.*

Pressure on the balls of my feet against the soles of my shoes connected with each step to the second level. The weapon on the belt concealed under my jacket slid out of the holster and stuck in the dampness of my palm.

Back flat against the wall. Search for movement. Listen. Street sounds and the thrum of heartbeat in my ears.

I rounded the corner. Heard the scrape on cement. Saw broad shoulders hunched over bent knees and a long narrow metal box. In the cover of thick pillars supporting the floor above, I edged closer to observe him. Large hands lifted a rifle stock and barrel from the open box.

An M14 can be assembled in minutes. I broke cover and shifted my feet to tactical stance.

Feet shoulder width apart. Square to the target. Knees bent.

His laugh rumbled deep in his chest. "I know you're there, Smart Alec." Rifle parts clicked into place. "What are you going to do? Blow holes in an unarmed man?"

You know I won't, you son of a bitch! "You load that rifle, you're armed. It's between you and me now."

Your call. Your move.

"Don't flatter yourself." Mobley stood.

He's taller. Stronger. But I have the advantage.

"Hands where I can see them."

Mobley mounted and adjusted the scope on the rifle. "Truth is what's between you and me is only one cog in a wheel that can't be stopped." He gripped the now fully assembled rifle.

My earpiece crackled a heads-up message. "Limo has arrived."

Tell him! Now! "He's not in the car, Mobley."

No reaction.

"The PM is safe at home."

"You're lying."

"Am I? You've got eyes. How many vehicles?"

No reply.

"With all the noise against the handgun ban why doesn't the PM have more protection? Where's the rest of his detail?"

Let that sink in.

"Any movement yet from the limo? Doors opening? Has anyone come out of the office to greet him?"

Play the hand.

"Why not, huh? Riddle me that, Joker."

"Fuck you!" Mobley slammed the rifle to the ground. "I busted your balls at the academy. This is how I beat you at role play. It was my finest moment in an RCMP uniform. Remember that, Smart Alec?"

Yeah. I remember. "Officer needs assistance," I said into the earpiece mic. "Second level parking garage."

Fingers on the hands behind his head in surrender knotted to fists. "You're not even man enough to take me out on your own."

"I'm doing my job. I follow procedure. You never did." I inched toward him, gun drawn until I got close enough to kick the rifle away. The skid of metal merged with the scuff of a small army of shoes on cement.

Here comes the cavalry. I holstered my sidearm and cuffed him as back up arrived.

Colin nodded to the officers that led Mobley away. "You must have figured out what was missing," he said.

Always watch your back, Smart Alec. He'd taunted me like Batman's villain. Laughed in my face when the instructor ended the exercise I'd failed. "I remembered how he beat me."

156

"Excuse me?"

"At the academy. Role play. Sniper scenario. I covered the front. He came at me from behind." I popped out and pocketed the earpiece. "Today I beat him."

Chapter 35

Tuesday the 18th - Jerilynn

Intense doesn't even begin to describe the frantic pace and level of tension the day before third reading in the House of Commons of the amendment to the law that would ban the sale and ownership of handguns. Time and my perception of it turned liquid somewhere around the top of the fourteenth consecutive hour in the office. Too exhausted to drive home, I called Alec. He arrived along with the RCMP detail that would escort the prime minister safely home to Rideau Cottage.

My rock. You kept your promise. Dinner was late last night but you were there.

Looking back through the blur of brain-fry exhaustion, I recall seeing the security guard who had come to my rescue in the parking lot when I'd worked late in December clearing my desk before the holidays. Willie had nearly frozen his ungloved hands connecting jumper cables from my car's battery to his. He refused my offer to pay him for his trouble. "No, Miss Connor," he'd said. "I'm happy to help." He blushed and stuttered his thanks when I came in early my first day back from break and gave him the pair of gloves I'd scored from a Boxing Day bargain table.

Willie jogged past us as he came to work on this night. A faded Toronto Maple Leafs jacket was draped over his arm. "Have a quiet night, Willie," I said.

"Thank you, Miss Connor," he replied. "Good night, sir." He acknowledged my husband and quickly rounded the nearest corner.

"That's odd," I said to Alec. "He's not a great conversationalist. But he usually asks how I am or how my day was. Is he late for work?"

Alec checked his watch. "No. He's a half hour early for night shift. What's his name?"

"Willie Carlyle. I asked to make sure he got the gloves I bought to thank him for starting my car."

Alec unlocked the car and opened the door for me. "Well, I've never had a complaint about him. Comes to work. Does his job. My kind of employee."

Chapter 36

Henry and Willie

An emotional miasma of agitation, confusion and anger had commandeered Henry's usual laid back approach to life. He grumbled his displeasure to Willie over cups of coffee and his deck of cards on the break room table.

"The thing is I can't remember when I would have gone out the back door and left it unlocked."

Willie concentrated on the stirred powdered creamer that swirled in his cup. "You did take out the trash while I was there."

"Yeah, but I've done that hundreds of times in the thirty years I've lived in that house. I've never left that door unlocked." Henry shuffled the deck of cards and slapped the jack of clubs on the table. "Cop sense doesn't turn off on the last day of service. What was taken was too specific for random theft. My watch. The gold badge I got when I retired. The ruby ring my late wife gave me on our twenty-fifth anniversary. Still there. Only my gun and this," he tapped the card with his finger, "were missing."

Willie swallowed his coffee and his nerves. "What do you think it means?" he asked.

"The gun is valuable and has an obvious use. The card could be a clue." Henry shook his head. "But I don't have a clue what it means. Yet." He grimaced at the apparent foul taste of his coffee and abandoned what was left in the cup. "I'm heading out." The legs of the chair scraped the floor. Henry left Willie to worry and plot his next move.

He'll put it together sooner rather than later. I've got to do this. Soon.

Chapter 37

Wednesday the 19th - Jerilynn

After a restless night of running checklists in my head, Alec dropped me off on Parliament Hill at seven thirty the next morning and continued on to his weekly meeting with the RCMP Commissioner. The prime minister was already in his office.

"Good morning, boss," I said.

"Jerilynn," he beckoned me in with the hand holding the pen, the other pressed the desk phone receiver to his ear. *"Ce n'est pas un compromis acceptable,"* he told the caller. *"Vous connaissez les termes."*

"A fight to the finish," I said when he returned the phone handset to the cradle.

"Yes, and we're nowhere close to the end I'm afraid." He collected the pile of documents in need of corrections. "I'm a bit surprised the Bloc Quebecois is pushing back harder than the Conservatives. They're all good with the assault weapon buyback but not so much on banning handguns entirely." He leaned back in the chair and rubbed his closed eyelids. "What I wouldn't give for a good night's sleep."

"My Dad thinks sleep is a waste of time. 'I'll sleep when I'm dead,' he'd say."

Although that had not been my intent, I was pleased when he laughed. "That option is way too permanent," he said. "Speaking of options, I'd best warn Carla that I may have to leave the House of Commons before the end of session. I've got to get home at a reasonable hour tonight. It's Gabrielle's thirteenth birthday. If I'm not there when she blows out the candles on her cake it could do irreparable harm to my marriage."

I sensed no humour in what had to be a concern expressed in jest without basis in fact. Their hours apart had been long and lately the tension had been ridiculously high. But he and Angeline were as rock solid as Alec and I. He didn't really mean what he'd said. Or did he? Was that the reason why he'd taken a personal day?

The desk phone rang with what I assumed would continue the compromise discussion I'd walked in on. I took the papers that needed my attention and got to work preparing the prime minister for the third and final round of the gun bill battle.

Four hours, a light lunch, and a thirty minute press briefing later, my boss and I were headed for the House of Commons.

Chapter 38

Alec

I got back from my weekly meeting with Commissioner Burke burdened by the usual priority list of operations marching orders, in-basket file folder overflow, an email backlog and a call from the Speaker of the House of Commons.

"We're expecting quite a crowd here this afternoon," he said.

Yeah, tell me something I don't know, Mr. Speaker. In the interest of job security, I kept that comment to myself. "I assure you every precaution will be taken and the appropriate uniformed personnel have been assigned."

"I expect so." Mister man-of-few-words ended the call.

The crush of protesters we'd prepared for based on the number of permits filed hadn't happened. Respectable numbers of people with hand-drawn homemade placards glued on thin sticks of spindly wood marched around The Hill. Shouts that warned of democracy lost to dictatorship and treason assaulted the ears. Pre-printed flyers shoved into hands that that didn't want them littered the ground. But the assembly was otherwise peaceful. No one brought a gun.

The districts reported no new activity that could disrupt the gun bill vote. With the detention, questioning and Crown charges opposing bail for Manning and Duvall and Mobley certain to rot in a federal penitentiary for conspiring to assassinate the prime minister, the external threat seemed neutralized for now.

What was it Mobley said about he and I being cogs in a wheel that can't be stopped? What the hell did he mean by that? How many cogs are in that wheel? Who built the machine? Where is the money coming from to power it? I rubbed my temples to clear the anxiety raised by questions for later days. A remote check-in with my officers on the foyer floor outside the House of Commons would suffice for now. *They know their jobs. They don't need me swimming in their soup.*

Chapter 39

Jerilynn

Activity outside the West Block doors to the House of Commons churned heavier than usual with visitors and crews from domestic and foreign media attracted to the possibility of witnessing history. Members of Parliament assembled ahead of the bell. Staff and ministers exchanged muted instructions over the chatter of voices and click and shuffle of high heels and leather soles on the polished floor.

I checked the prime minister's papers one last time and handed over the folder, satisfied the contents met our mutual satisfaction. "Good luck," I said and turned back toward my office for a much needed cup of coffee. The path of people ahead cleared. A man in a faded Toronto Maple Leaf jacket stepped into the opening. He stopped, set his feet in a stance I'd seen in Alec's RCMP training videos, and reached inside his jacket. The barrel of the gun raised and pointed behind and over my shoulder.

"NO!" I screamed and pivoted toward the intended target. The projectile fired in the blast behind me whistled past my right ear. The dull thud and guttural cry pierced my heart. The jolt as my knees, hip and left elbow hit the floor collapsed my soul. I wiped blood from my face and prayed it was only mine.

My prayer was not answered.

"Evan!" I crawled to him, stared in horror at the size of the hole in his jacket and the blood that had soaked his white shirt red. My hand on his chest felt no movement. "Evan! Breathe! Please breathe!" The plea left my throat as a whimper.

"Move, Jerilynn. I've got this."

I sat back on my heels and tried to identify the middle-aged woman in a grey suit. *Is she a visitor? A reporter? Staff? An MP?* I winced as she ripped away what covered his wound. Blood gushed from the hole in his flesh. I rocked on my knees and sobbed into my fist.

My fractured mind pieced together and connected the face to the voice. *Margot.* Her signature silk scarf accessory wadded as a compress under the hard press of her fingers. The flow of blood slowed. He moaned and tried to twist away.

"You're going to be fine, Prime Minister," I heard her say.

Reassurance rebooted my memory. *She's a doctor. She'll save him.*

A wave of RCMP officers and medical first responders surrounded us. Margot took over the scene. "Don't touch her!" she commanded. "Vital signs," she demanded. Medics responded. "BP 100 over 60. Pulse 132." Margot plugged the tips of a borrowed stethoscope into her ears and pressed the diaphragm to his chest. "Lungs clear. Breath sounds bilateral." *Is this really happening?* I watched from where I'd crawled to, out of sight and out of the way. Aware yet not, able to move but frozen for what seemed like hours. *What's that sound?* I clamped my teeth together to stop the chatter. Hugged myself to quell the shake.

"Jerilynn. Can you hear me? Are you alright?"

The usually crowded foyer appeared mostly deserted, the familiar seen for the first time. *Where had everyone gone?* I shifted my confusion to focus on Margot. "Where is Evan?" I asked her.

"The Prime Minister is on his way to hospital," she answered.

"He's alive?"

"Very much so." I could tell by the probing stare and once over scan that she was evaluating my condition. An RCMP officer hovered above us. "Call for a second ambulance," she told him.

I protested. She insisted. "You're in shock and you need stitches in your bottom lip."

My fingers touched the puffy spot sticky with a trickle of fresh over dried blood. "How did this happen?"

165

Her closed lips turned up to half-smile. "You most likely bit your lip when you tackled the prime minister."

"I didn't."

"Oh, yes you did." Her smile vanished. "You may have saved his life."

"Not me. You did that."

"I did what I'm trained to do. You reacted and put yourself at risk." Margot stepped away to let the medics do their work. I reached for her hand as the gurney wheels under me began to roll.

"Would you like me to go with you?"

"Yes. Please."

Waves of panic battered my frail hold on reality. Her hand was the lifeline that kept me from going under.

Chapter 40

Alec

The interoperable communications system alerting RCMP, Ottawa Police, plainclothes security detail and uniformed guards in the House of Commons sounded halfway through lunch at my desk.

"Active shooter in the West Block! Foyer outside House of Commons!"

Oh hell no! "Lockdown The Hill. No one in or out." I ordered a planned systematic enforcement of trained responses. The first and second lines of defense along Wellington Street and the Peace Tower would be in place. The third layer of officers would shut down all entrances, offices, corridors and vulnerable areas within the parliamentary precinct.

My back yard.

I holstered my sidearm, grabbed earpiece and cell phone, and ran toward the West Block. Transmitted reports from the targeted site confirmed the efficiency of our unified security force.

"Suspect down."

"Parliamentarians secure in House of Commons."

"Staff secure in offices."

"Visitors and media secure in meeting rooms."

"Number of victims?" I asked.

"One. The prime minister."

Fuck! How? Who? I dodged the thinning pack of people exhibiting varying degrees of shock and panic being led down the corridor to lockdown safety. Duty required that I cease and resist any and all emotional reaction to the ground zero scene under my command.

The apparent shooter was face down on the floor, hands cuffed behind his back, the weapon out of his reach. A gloved RCMP officer bent down, recovered and bagged it. Medics rolled the gurney that would transport the prime minister to the ambulance and on to hospital. Boots and shoes tracked and smeared the floor with blood from the puddle pooled two meters away from the House of Commons doors.

"Full sweep," I ordered and joined my officers in a painstaking search of the West Block for other shooters or accomplices. Every corridor cleared and door opened, exit checked and window intact confirmed what I was certain we wouldn't find. Instincts honed in training and job experience dismissed suspicion and the possibility of any other explanation or motive. The guy in the Maple Leafs jacket, lifted from the floor by my officers and on his way to the Ottawa Police lock up, had acted on his own to assassinate Evan Reid.

"Sir, this was found on the floor near the scene." The uniformed security guard handed me a cell phone in a cracked case. "It belongs to the prime minister's chief of staff."

The gnawing feeling that something was not quite right ratcheted up fear I fought to control. *My wife is never without her phone. She had to be here when the prime minister was shot.* I thanked him and called the prime minister's office.

"No, I'm sorry she's not here." Jerilynn's assistant struggled to control the sob and fright in her voice. "She didn't come back to the office. Last we heard she went with the prime minister."

Concern replaced the initial rush of relief. My wife wasn't physically injured. But how would she react to and process the trauma of what she'd witnessed? I called Colin, operations officer in command at hospital. "Yes, your wife is here," he said. "She's with the prime minister's family."

"What's the report on his condition?"

"Critical. He's in surgery."

Dammit! What did I miss? This is on me! My angry blame game and conversation with Colin was cut short by an incoming call from the Ottawa police.

Chapter 41

Jerilynn

Margot stayed with me through the emergency room question and answer poke and prod. I forced myself back from dazed and confused to concentrate on talking through the swelling in my lip and numbing effect of local anesthetic that affected my speech. Anyone in scrubs and white lab coats had the same answer to my obvious question.

"The prime minister is in surgery," was all they would or quite possibly could tell me.

"It's been hours," I lamented to Margot.

"Actually, no," she replied. "He's only been in surgery for a little over an hour. That's not unusual at all with gunshot wounds. How are you feeling?"

"To be honest, I'm not sure yet."

"He asked about you."

The woman sitting on the bench beside me was disheveled in an out-of-the-ordinary way. The precision cut layers of her collar-length salt-and-pepper brunette hair hung in unruly waves. Her suit and white blouse were streaked with blood. I wondered what I'd see when I looked in the mirror.

"He wanted to know if you were OK and if anyone else had been hurt." Margot felt for the scarf that wasn't there. "He is a good man."

I reached for her hand and squeezed. "Now there's a first. A Tory complimenting a Liberal."

She squeezed back. "Partisan nonsense."

The swarm of media and RCMP tasked with security in the midst of chaos moved closer. The clamor and buzz signaled a stoked feeding frenzy. The reason was revealed via a radioed heads-up call to the officers around us. The prime minister's family had arrived.

"I think I'd better go before I'm seen," Margot said.

"You definitely don't want to be caught on camera or quoted," I said.

"You are right about that."

"How will you get back to Parliament Hill?"

"I'll get a cab. Will you be OK?"

"I'll be fine. My husband will probably be here soon. I should see to the family."

"Uh, you might want to clean up a bit before you do that."

With the blinders of shock removed, I looked down and saw why. Although my hands had been cleaned in the emergency room, dried blood had caked beneath my clear polished fingernails and streaked the fabric of my pale yellow suit jacket. My blouse was no longer white.

"Let me take your jacket with me. I'll drop it off at the cleaners."

I took it off, handed it over and hugged her. "Thank you. For everything." I escaped into the nearest washroom.

Margot had gotten away just in time.

I heard Celine Reid in the hallway outside the washroom door. "Where is my son?" The tremor of near hysteria in her cry underscored the urgency to comfort her. I walked into the epicenter of the uniformed entourage anticipating Alec's help.

No such luck.

"Jerilynn!" The prime minister's mother let go of Angeline and reached out to me then retracted her hands and stepped back. Her hands over her mouth covered a silent scream. I'd done my best to sponge blood from my blouse with soap from a dispenser and paper towels. But the evidence of violence remained.

Hospital security ushered us into an empty waiting room. The RCMP closed ranks at and beyond the door both to block entry and ensure privacy. Angeline gently led Celine to sit beside her. The women who loved him huddled on a drab institutional green faux leather couch. I completed the anxious circle, seated on the edge of an equally utilitarian chair.

"Have you heard anything?" Angeline asked me. The drawn pinch of panic in her eyes contrasted and betrayed the forced control in her voice.

"He's in surgery. That's all I know."

"How could this happen to my beautiful boy?" Celine's shoulders shook with the effort of breath forming words. "Who did this? Why? I need to know why." Trembling fingers kneaded the couch cushion. "Does Jonathan know? Angeline, did you call him?"

"Yes, I talked to him. He was already at the airport waiting on a flight out of Christchurch. He'll be here tomorrow."

"Good. That's good." Celine seemed to be talking to calm herself. "Jonathan will know what to do. He always has. Just like his father. Did you know we named him for his grandfather? He was the premier of British Columbia. I was so sure Jonathan would be a premier or maybe even prime minister like Tony." Her palm patted my knee. "Did you know my husband? Of course you wouldn't. He's been gone, oh, how many years now?" Her outward expressions of desperation softened as she stopped to remember. "He had a funny lopsided smile and a way of winking at me just so that made me smile, too. Evan seemed happy, so content to be a teacher. I was surprised when he came back to Ottawa. Then again, he'd met you, dear one." She patted Angeline's knee. "It was love at first sight, you know. Jonathan knows his brother. I asked him why he didn't ask you out. He told me he was saving you for Evan."

The door opened. A man of color in green scrubs, surgical mask loose around his neck, strode into the room on shoes still covered in paper held by elastic. "Mrs. Reid?" Angeline stood. Celine reached for and held on to her daughter-in-law's hand. "I am Dr. Etienne. The surgery went very well," he said in a lilting blend of French and Creole slightly North Americanized from his likely Haitian homeland.

"Can we see him?" Celine's nervous rambling had apparently drained her. I wasn't sure if the surgeon had heard her weak request.

He stepped forward, bent his knees, balanced on the balls of his feet and spoke to Celine from her eye level. "Your son is in recovery. If all continues to go well, he will be moved to intensive care within the hour."

"If all goes well?" Her hollow echo of his words was even less audible.

"He is a strong and healthy man. The wound was serious, yes. But the bullet caused no permanent damage." Dr. Etienne stood tall. His confident presence convinced me that my boss, my friend, would survive. "I will come back to get you when my patient is ready for visitors."

"Thank you, Doctor," Angeline said and sank back on the couch cushion beside Celine. A degree of relief turned her attention outward and toward me. "What happened to you?" she asked.

"That's a long story."

"It would appear that you have time to tell it," Angeline said.

"So it would," I said and shared edited details of a dreadful afternoon. I deliberately left out the horrifying bits that I didn't yet have the words to describe.

Dr. Etienne returned about two hours later. "There is a problem," he said.

My heart dropped to the pit of my empty stomach. Celine wrapped her arms around her body, closed her eyes tight and prayed out loud. Angeline's face went pale. I caught her as she swayed on legs that threatened to fold.

"The Prime Minister is not responding. He should have regained consciousness. He has not."

I forced my question past the lump in my throat that I could not swallow. "What can we do?"

"Come with me."

I kept my arm around Angeline and reached for Celine. She took my hand. Somehow, the three of us walked through the door and down endless corridors past a legion of RCMP officers to his private room bedside in ICU.

Monitors that tracked his life signs blipped and beeped. Bottoms up bags of intravenous fluids dripped saline solution into tubes funneled to a needle embedded in his vein. His chest rose and fell without assistance. But the vibrant force that orchestrated and conducted a G7 economy and led a country of thirty million people lie dormant and silent between the raised metal rails of a hospital bed.

"Evan. My beautiful boy." Celine went to him and sat in the chair beside him. She reached through the rails and tenderly touched his cheek. "Please, please open your eyes."

Tears and her plaintive plea weren't getting through. *I knew what would. A man of strength will respond to strength.*

A shared glance with Angeline told me she knew that, too. She stood over her husband at the side of the bed opposite his mother. "Wake up, Evan!" she demanded in a stern, steady voice.

The immediate reaction rippled from his quick intake of breath to the gradual opening and blink of his eyelids. His lips parted and moved to form a single barely-above-whispered word. "Angeline."

"Welcome back, my love," she said and lightly kissed his lips.

I took my cue to discretely back away from a very personal family moment. "Don't cry Mum," I heard him say as the door closed softly behind me.

Each footstep from ICU to the nearest exit sign brought me closer to the realization that I had no plan for a way home. Not a man or woman in the RCMP contingent lining the hallway looked at all familiar to me. I knew any of the officers would give me a ride. All I had to do was ask.

You pulled out all the stops and assembled the troops. But where were you when I really needed you, Alec?

I immediately shamed myself for this petulant accusation. The lives of everyone on Parliament Hill were my husband's responsibility. I'd done what I could to save one. Knowing his likely state of professional angst and self-inflicted hell over an incident and outcome he couldn't control tempered the flare of my selfish accusation. I crumpled onto a bench outside the surgical waiting room and cradled my head in my hands to counter the weight of exhaustion.

We need each other now, love. Where are you?

Chapter 42

Evan

I hadn't slept much the night before. Even less than what seemed to be my new normal of four to five hours. That's when the restless whir in my brain pounded on my eyelids until I gave up on sleep. But I do remember the dream.

I'd doubled down on the campaign for my first bicycle the day after I didn't get one for Christmas. I saved up my allowance money to pay for a subscription to Bicycling Magazine and cut out pictures of preferred models. Mum found those pictures in her purse, the laundry basket, between recipes in her binder and the pages of whatever book she was reading. Dad joked about being halfway through a speech in the House of Commons and turning the page on a full-sized photo of a silver BMX freestyle built for speed on any surface.

The school year ended, the weather got warm and my strategy produced the desired reward on Canada Day, my eighth birthday. Mum fretted when Dad and I rejected her request to install training wheels. "Nonsense," said Dad in the rumbling tone that made MPs on both sides of the aisle take notice. "Our son will learn the proper way to ride on two wheels." The abbreviated summer schedule on Parliament Hill gave us time for him to guide me with his strong hands around my waist. I'd pump the pedals. He'd cheer me on and let go. Every day I'd make it a bit further down the driveway before the bike would begin to wobble. He was always there to catch me.

A month into the lessons, I decided to have a go on my own. I wheeled my bike out, straddled the seat, took my sneakered feet off the pavement, and pedaled. The breeze lifted my spirits and the Toronto Blue Jays cap from my head. I'd done it! My silver symbol of freedom would take me wherever I wanted to go! The wheels turned, the bike picked up speed and in a split second of paralyzing fear, I forgot how to apply the brakes. The exhilaration of accomplishment ended in the blast from a car horn, the screech of tires on cement, my Mum's high-pitched scream and the worst pain I'd ever felt until a bullet ripped into my shoulder.

I've heard that scenes of sudden traumatic events play out in slow motion in the minds' eye of victims and witnesses. Not so in my experience. Jerilynn walked with me to the doors of the House of Commons. I flipped through the papers she handed me and heard the bell ring summoning parliamentarians to the sitting. In split second sequence, she turned her head away, cried out a single word warning and shoved me at the exact moment the sound of a fired handgun echoed in my ears and the brutal force of the bullet jolted me backward. I dropped to the floor.

All the hazy images after appear in a slide show distorted by intense burning agony. Jerilynn, her face spattered with blood – mine, hers, or both I couldn't be sure - calling my name, pleading with me to breathe. A woman I vaguely recognized as the opposition party MP I'd chastised my chief of staff for befriending, tearing at the clothing over the wound, pressing hard into the center of my pain. I know now she was doing what she could to slow blood loss. But at the time, I just wanted her to stop. I remember asking her if Jerilynn was OK, if anyone else was hurt. She said no one else had been shot, Jerilynn was not injured and you're going to be fine, Prime Minister.

It was then that the mercifully numbing black curtain of lost consciousness fell. No pain. No fear. Only infinite and timeless nothing.

Time and place had lost measure and context. Someone asked me my name and if I knew where I was or what had happened. I tried to answer. But my throat was parched and my lips wouldn't move.

A distinctive deep voice spoke to me in French. "*Vous m'entendez, M. le Premier Ministre?*" he said. Do you hear me, Prime Minister? "*Oui, je vous entends, je ne peux pas vous parler.*" Yes, I hear you but I can't tell you. The words were there but in thought only. I heard Mum crying and Dad telling her not to, that my life and purpose for living it was far from over. My reason for living called me out from the darkness.

"Wake up, Evan!"

The curtain lifted. I drifted toward the glow on the other side, forced my eyes to open and once more fell in love with the most beautiful woman I would ever know.

"Angeline." My brittle voice crackled just above a whisper.

"Welcome back, my love." Her soft kiss took the last of the hurt away.

Chapter 43

William

Intercom buzz on the desk phone of William Carlyle, attorney at law, sounded in harsh harmony to the wail of sirens that seemed to converge from all directions. He glanced out the window at the rapid pass of rhythmic red light flashes and picked up the phone.

"Yes."

"Your wife is on line three."

Whatever she wants it must be serious, he thought. *She knows better than to call with anything less trivial than the house is on fire. He pressed the blinking white light.* "Yes, Rose. What is it?"

"Willie didn't come home from work this morning."

The drum of his fingers on the desk top both expressed and expelled his annoyance. "What do you want me to do about it? Hunt him down?"

"There's been a shooting on Parliament Hill. It's on the news right now on the radio. I'm worried about Willie."

Another shooting? I thought we imposed that layer of taxpayer funded bureaucracy eight years ago to keep this from happening again. William left clicked the mouse under his palm, first on the Internet icon and again on the CBC icon. Breaking News reported a shooting near the House of Commons. The anchor's voice reported over live video of officers in RCMP uniforms hustling people to safety, medics attending to a victim and a suspect face down on the floor, hands cuffed behind his back.

"Bill? Are you still there?"

"Yes, Rose. I'm watching CBC News."

"Are they saying who has been shot?"

"Not yet, no."

"I'm frightened, Bill."

He looked at the clock on the wall opposite the desk. "Willie's shift ended hours ago. I doubt if he's still in the building." At that moment, the gurney rolled past the camera. Although the medics tried to shield the victim and his identity, William knew immediately from the profile under the oxygen mask to the distinctive reddish-brown color of his hair.

It was Evan Reid.

"Holy God. The Prime Minister has been shot."

"Oh no!" Rose began to sob in wretched, ragged breaths.

RCMP officers on either side of the suspect hauled the man in handcuffs to his feet. William had threatened to throw out that faded Maple Leafs jacket with the crescent moon tear on the right shoulder every time he failed to find an empty hanger in the coat closet.

No! It can't be. The unthinkable conclusion screamed in his head.

"Rose, I gotta go."

"But what about Willie?"

"I'll call you as soon as I know something." He hung up the phone and hurried toward the chaos on Parliament Hill. The panicked crowd of retreating protesters impeded his progress. William slipped on a forgotten sign and stumbled on an uncut curb. An officer in RCMP uniform and flak jacket helped him back to his feet.

"Are you OK, sir?" the officer asked at the exact moment an RCMP cruiser with lights flashing and siren blaring inched a cautious path from the West Block onto Wellington Street. The man in back stared straight ahead. The profile was William's mirror image.

He kept pace with the flow of the frightened to his car parked in a spot marked reserved. A less travelled route along residential side streets bypassed main artery snarl. His luxury sedan beat out a VW with mismatched color doors for the last visitor spot in the Ottawa PD parking lot.

The hounds of media rabid for exclusive quotes and video had broken away from the pack outside Parliament Hill. William watched from a distance as his only son was escorted under public scrutiny from the marked car through the doors he knew led to suspect processing and eventual lock up. He skirted the mob and scene and waited for an opportunity to discretely slip through the main doors. Once inside, he elbowed his way to the front desk and pounded his fist to garner attention.

"Yes, sir?" A uniformed female officer held and covered the receiver of a multi-line phone with her palm.

"I demand to see my son."

"Your name, sir?"

"William Carlyle Senior, attorney at law."

"One moment, sir." The officer completed a brief conversation and hung up the handset. "Please have a seat. My CO will be with you shortly." The officer turned her back to William and picked up the handset. William's face flushed crimson. His complaints grew louder.

"I will not be ignored!" William roared over the din.

Chapter 44

Alec

William Carlyle was demanding to see the suspect in lock up. It seems Willie Carlyle, night shift security, the soft-spoken, polite, mouse of a boy in a man's body had smuggled a gun onto Parliament Hill and fired a bullet into our prime minister.

Go figure.

The task of handling the pissed off former MP and his accused son had fallen on my shoulders. Carlyle the Elder had been ushered into a smaller room away from the ebb and flow of daily police business.

"I'm Chief Superintendent Alec Martin."

"Yes, I know who you are. Director of Parliamentary Protective Service. I was one of the MPs who voted to create the job that gave you that title."

"What is your name, sir?"

"You know very well who I am."

"I need you to tell me."

"William Carlyle. My son William Carlyle Junior is on your payroll. I pulled the strings that put him there."

"William Carlyle Junior is in RCMP custody for the attempted assassination of Prime Minister Evan Reid."

"Ridiculous."

"No, sir. Your son was apprehended by my officers at the scene."

"I demand to see him at once."

"Are you his counsel?"

"I am an attorney as well as his father!"

"Very well." I alerted lock up that a visitor would be escorted by me to maximum security. "This way, sir."

Ballasts of institutional overhead lights called attention to every crack and paint peel in the dismal hallway. Heavy doors swung open and clanked closed. Willie sat on the mattress of a single bunk bed covered by sheets and an olive green blanket in a cell far removed from the rest of the incarcerated. Emotionless glazed-over eyes looked up at me, then to his father, and back to the concrete floor.

"Do you mind?" William dismissed me with more than words. "I'd like to talk with my son in private."

"You've got ten minutes." I unlocked the cell, opened the door wide enough to admit the father, and locked them both in.

Chapter 45

William and Willie

Father and son stayed silent until the sound of footsteps receded and the cell block door closed.

William paced the floor in front of Willie from the bars to the smooth white cement block cell wall. Willie's calm contrasted sharply with his father's agitation.

"This is very important, William. Have you said anything to the RCMP? Did you ask to call a lawyer?"

"No."

"Good. That's good. I'll see what I can do about this absurd accusation and get you out of here."

"I shot him."

William froze in his tracks. He closed the distance between them and invaded Willie's space.

"You did WHAT?"

"I shot the Prime Minister."

"Are you OUT OF YOUR MIND?" The father fisted the fabric shoulders of his son's shirt and lifted Willie from the bunk to his feet. "For the love of God, WHY?"

"So you would stop yelling." Willie shrugged out of his father's grasp. "Every morning when I got home from work. Every night at the dinner table. You shout at Mom. You shout at Annabel and Fiona. And at me." He pointed a finger to his chest and continued in a flat emotionless monotone. "You tell us how much you hate being a lawyer, that all you ever wanted was to be a Member of Parliament. Every day since you lost the first election. Every day since the voters didn't put you back where you wanted to be. Every day for almost eight years we've had to hear you say how much you hate Evan Reid. That you'd still be in the House of Commons if it wasn't for him and his Liberal Party. That he had to go. I couldn't take it anymore." Willie's hardened gaze stared into his father's eyes. "So I got Henry to show me how to use a gun. I was gonna make the prime minister go away for good so you would stop yelling at us."

William groaned, sat on the bunk next to his son and dropped his head into his hands.

Willie moved as far from his father as the meager mattress would allow. "Is he still alive?

"What? Who?"

"The Prime Minister. Is he still alive?"

"To my knowledge, yes."

"That's too bad. I mean I didn't want him to suffer. Henry told me getting shot hurts real bad. He taught me how to aim for center mass. Dead center, he called it. The bullet hits the heart. I practiced at the range and I got really good at it. He would have died before he hit the floor. Miss Connor got in the way.

I didn't want to hurt her. She's always been nice to me."

The father gripped the mattress with his fists and stared at the floor. "What are you telling me, William? Where did you get the gun?"

"It's Henry's gun."

"You stole a gun with the sole intent to kill a man?"

"I didn't steal it. I borrowed it."

"How were you going to return it from a prison cell?"

Willie shrugged. "The RCMP has it now, right? They'll give it back to Henry when they're done with it."

"Oh my God," William groaned again. "I can't believe this. How? How could …?" He struggled to make sense of a hell that until this moment he couldn't have imagined. "Civilized people live according to the laws and values of our democracy. We obey the law. We vote. We don't resolve our differences by taking a man's life. I cannot believe that my bitterness at losing a seat in the House of Commons caused all of this." He got to his feet, walked to the locked cell door, and gripped the bars. "I've failed you. I've failed as a father and as a man and the consequences of that failure may cost another man and father his life." He touched his forehead to the unforgiving metal. "I've lost my son. All I can do now is pray that Celine Reid won't lose hers." Even the bars and walls of the maximum security cell couldn't contain his torment.

Alec's footsteps of return signaled an end to a tortured exchange of truths and consequences. "Mr. Carlyle, your ten minutes are up."

William let go of the bars. Alec opened the cell door.

Willie stood and faced an officer of the law on the other side of the bars that confined him. "I want to call a lawyer now," he told Alec.

"I'll arrange it."

William stiffened. "I guess we're done here." He flinched when the cell door closed.

Chapter 46

Alec

I don't believe in fate. But I couldn't help compare the parallel stories of fathers and sons caught up in the successes and snares of Ottawa politics. Prime Ministers Tony and Evan Reid shining examples of the former while the defeated Member of Parliament and Willie the security guard turned felon exemplified the latter.

Hours later, after the all-clear was declared, Parliament Hill re-opened. The media, unsatisfied with my guarded answers, packed up and trailed off to report more breaking news elsewhere. Finally, I was free to check on the welfare of my wife. I'd been informed a second ambulance had been dispatched to and from Parliament Hill for a victim with minor injuries. I was also relieved to know our prime minister was in serious but stable condition after surgery. I parked near but far enough away from a lower profile entrance to hospital in hope of avoiding more media attention.

Colin greeted me at the first floor elevator doors. "You must be very proud of your wife."

"Excuse me?"

"She stepped between the shooter and the prime minister. From what I've heard, if she hadn't, we'd more than likely be planning a state funeral." The emotional mix of shock, anger and a tinge of embarrassment must have been evident in my reaction. "I'm sorry. You didn't know?"

"I did not." I skipped the elevator and scaled the stairs two at a time to the floor marked ICU. I keyed my hand held radio. "Chief Superintendent Martin on my way up on foot to ICU. Open the stairway door." The sea of RCMP officers guarding the floor swept in then parted and stepped aside in deference to my rank and don't-fuck-with-me mood. Jerilynn stood in the middle of the hallway, her clothes blood-stained, her white-blond hair a disheveled mop over blood-shot eyes.

"Where have you been?" Words through the bruised and swollen lower lip pout on the injured love of my life spewed out in a pitch close to teenage girl whine.

"Locking down Parliament Hill and locking up the guy who tried to kill your boss," I said. "And what's this bullshit about you playing hero?"

"Somebody had to get between the gun and the prime minister."

"That's my job!"

"You weren't there!"

We sparred like competitors in the ring when we should have been holding each other. I made the first move. "I know. I should have been. I'm sorry." I closed the gap between us, opened my arms, and gently pulled her in against the open jacket of my uniform. "I'm so sorry, honey." Her open palms feebly slapped my chest. She sobbed, then sagged, the fight gone, the fear released in a torrent of tears and the occasional hiccup. I stroked her hair and kissed the top of head that fit neatly next to my heart as we knew it should and always would. "Don't ever do anything like that again," I said.

"I hope I never have to." She wiped her nose on the back of her hand and her face on my shirt.

"How is the prime minister?"

"He's going to be OK."

"Thank God for that. How is his family holding up?"

"Doing better now that he's conscious and talking. Angeline and Celine are here. His children aren't."

"The detail assigned to the kids took them from school to Rideau Cottage when The Hill locked down." I reached into my jacket pocket, retrieved her phone, and handed it to her. "A security guard found this."

"Oh!" She patted a pocket that wasn't there. "It must have fallen out of my jacket."

"Where is your jacket, honey?"

"Margot has it."

"How did Margot …"

"Long story."

"Tell me later." My arm around her steered us toward the elevators. "Let's go home."

Chapter 47

May ~ Alec

The Incident Report Commission wasted no time chairing up and loading their blame throwers. Within seventy-two hours, the pressure on Commissioner Burke to stand and report with whatever minions she assembled forced a scheduled appearance before the mixed political party bag of MPs and the Speakers of the House and Senate twelve days after the shooting. The media did their part to fan the flames with incendiary headlines.

RCMP Under Fire! Insider Plots Assassination.

How Did This Happen <u>Again</u>?

And my personal favorite.

The Parliamentary Protective Service That Isn't.

Great.

My department chased down and interviewed every credible witness, transcribed testimony into notes and produced an eighty-five page report complete with timelines, statistics, graphs, photos and alternative outcome scenarios. We walked into Canada's version of the Warren Commission hearings confident that we could answer any questions, grateful that unlike our American counterparts charged with investigating what went horribly wrong in Dallas, Texas on November 22, 1963, the leader of our government had survived.

"Thank you for answering our request to appear today, Commissioner Burke." Asad Bashir, House leader and chair of these proceedings, called the meeting to order. He turned over the first page of his copy of the report and nodded apparent approval. "We appreciate the care and effort required to provide us with what appears to be a comprehensive account of the investigation."

"Thank you, Mr. Chairman," Commissioner Burke replied. "It is our pleasure and privilege to summarize the contents of the report and answer all questions to the best of our knowledge and ability. Before we proceed, I would like to introduce Director of Parliamentary Protective Service Chief Superintendent Alec Martin and Director of Operations Colin Landry."

"*Pouvez-vous répéter?*" The Bloc Quebecois MP had made his presence and official language preference known.

"*Bien sûr,*" she replied, did so, and then repeated in French all that she said in English. "As the commanding officer, Chief Martin was in charge of the investigation and the events leading up to the incident at the doors of the House of Commons on Wednesday, April nineteenth."

That was my cue.

"Thank you, Commissioner." A complete account and full disclosure of everything written and diagramed between the pages of the report consumed the next hour. Since my fluency in French leaves much to be desired, I relied almost entirely on the commissioner to translate when asked and Colin to fill in the details in both languages as needed.

"Point of order!" A thin man in a suit and tie as black as his slicked back hair and a shirt as white as his pasty skin tried to stare me down through pop bottle bottom thick lenses in black rimmed frames.

"Chair recognizes Mr. Kingston Poirier," said Chairman Bashir.

"Why is it that the Director of Parliamentary Protective Service is not fluent in both official languages of Canada?"

Who is this dickhead? I thought.

"The question has no relevance to the investigation or the contents of the report," the chairman ruled. "Ask another question, Mr. Poirier."

"My apologies, Mr. Chairman," Poirier replied and turned his attention back to me. "Director Martin, exactly when did you know with certainty that the gun used in the attempted assassination of the prime minister belonged to a member of the security staff?"

"As I said in my summary, licensed legal ownership of the handgun was traced to Henry Schaughnessy within two hours of the firearm's confiscation by the RCMP officers who took Mr. Carlyle into custody at the scene of the incident."

"Please, for the committee's edification, describe the requirements of licensed legal ownership."

"Legal ownership of a restricted firearm such as the Smith and Wesson 686 requires a possession and acquisition license and a registration certificate to the owner at the place of residence."

"In his official capacity as a security guard, was Mr. Schaughnessy required to carry a gun?"

"No, he was not."

"Did Mr. Schaughnessy have any other licenses or permits for his firearm?"

I knew where this was going. "Yes. He had an authorization to carry."

"Which means what?"

"The firearm could be transported for specific uses."

"Such as?"

"Point of order, Mr. Chairman," said Frank McInnis, who I recognized as the Liberal MP from my Nova Scotia hometown riding. "I fail to see the relevance of this line of questioning and Mr. Poirier's allotted time for questions must have expired by now."

"I'll allow this last question. But you are correct, Mr. McInnis. Mr. Poirier, you have asked your final question."

OK, Dickhead. You want an answer. Well, here it is.

"An authorization to carry allows the owner to transport the unloaded firearm for target practice or target shooting competition. The management of the range where the owner used his handgun for target practice reported that Mr. Schaughnessy always followed the law with regard to the safe transport and handling of his weapon. At this time I would like to reiterate that Mr. Schaughnessy is not under investigation. He reported his firearm stolen as soon as he discovered that it was missing from his residence. He voluntarily resigned from his position and is no longer employed as a security guard on Parliament Hill. I would also like to bring to the commission's attention the ammunition capacity and capability of the Smith and Wesson 686. As reported, the caliber bullet fired in the West Block on April nineteenth was standard pressure .38 special. This handgun also takes .357 magnum ammunition, which Mr. Schaughnessy told officers during the interview that he had never owned and would not use. If that higher velocity ammunition had been fired on the day of the incident the outcome would have in all likelihood been altered."

"Mr. Chairman, a question please."

"Go ahead, Mr. McInnis."

"Chief Superintendent Martin, this report mentions bullet trajectory. You've said the caliber of bullet would have made a difference in the outcome. What about the trajectory of the bullet had the prime minister's chief of staff not intervened?"

"Given the position of the gunman relative to the position of the prime minister, the probability of fatal outcome is ninety-eight percent."

Judging from the nervous shuffle, throat clearing and coughs, I'd made my point. I took the opportunity to make another.

"I am extremely proud of the efficient and exemplary response of every man and woman in uniform - RCMP, Ottawa PD, and Parliament Hill security personnel – on April nineteenth. We trained for it. We were ready for it. We followed protocols to the letter. What we were not ready for was an unforeseen internal threat. The exit door partially hidden by construction and the renovation of Centre Block that was accessed by Mr. Carlyle has been sealed. Every known point of entry and exit on Parliament Hill has been inspected and secured. We can mitigate risk. But we must always continue to look for ways to reduce risk even further. The job of all of us in this room is to do what we can to keep everyone as safe as is legally and humanly possible."

§

My wife treated me to dinner that night. She'd picked up a bottle of my favorite Argentina Malbec, twice-baked monster-sized potatoes, and grilled up a t-bone steak to my medium rare liking.

We ate by candlelight, sway-danced to soft saxophone jazz, and opened a second bottle of wine for a bedroom nightcap. The residual warmth of intimacy relaxed us to drift on the buoyant edge of doze. "What a dickhead," I said low and under my breath.

"Who are you talking about?"

"Sorry, honey, I thought you were asleep."

"I kinda was but I'm obviously not now." She rolled closer into my arms, one leg over mine and her head on my chest. "Who is the dickhead in question?"

"An MP who tried to seize his pathetic moment of imagined power by asking why I'm not fluent in French."

J-lynn snorted her 'you gotta be kidding me' laugh. "What's his name?"

"King something first name and a French-sounding last name."

"Kingston Poirier."

"Yeah, that's it. Face like a weasel. Thick lenses in Harry Potter frames. Probably can't see the end of his pointy nose without them." I buried my nose in her hair and kissed the top of her head. "I take it you know who I'm talking about."

"Tory in his fourth term. He gets a few more votes in his Barrie-Innisfil riding every election. He's been mentioned and backed away from party leadership a couple of times."

"Not a fan of your boss I'll wager."

"You'd win that bet."

"So why is he on the Incident Report Commission? He was more interested in hearing himself talk than asking questions about the incident or the report."

"You nailed the why, love. He grabs every chance he can to be on camera and make a lot of noise to get quoted in the media."

I felt the goosebumps rise as my fingers lightly stroked her arm. "I will never understand politicians. Too many of them are nothing but legal criminals."

"How do you mean?"

"I've staked my career on trying to outmaneuver the criminal mind. People who commit crimes inflict harm out of malice or jealousy. Anger or revenge. Or maybe just to see if they can get away with it. But politicians like this Poirier guy. They lie to people, tell them what they want to hear to get elected, then do the opposite and convince people it was for their own good or the good of the country. And they get re-elected so they can do it all over again. They don't give a damn about making policy or law or protecting people. They just want to hear themselves talk and strut around, fill their bank accounts any way they can, and do favors for assholes with even more money so they can con them into contributing to their re-election campaign."

"That's true for some. But definitely not the Prime Minister. I wouldn't be his chief of staff if it were."

"How is he doing?"

"He's still in hospital but he'll probably be released in the next couple of days."

"That's good news." Her silence told me she thought otherwise. "Something about that bothering you?"

"Well, yes and no. By all outward appearances, he is well on the road to recovery. Antibiotics did the trick. No infection. The wound is healing. He's still on pain meds and in physiotherapy. But that's to be expected. I've been with him when he's met with the deputy prime minister, the House leader and the minister of public safety. Except for the hospital room setting and what he's wearing, he is the Prime Minister."

"J-lynn." I rubbed her arm and covered her chill with a blanket. "You haven't answered my question."

She snuggled her shoulder under mine. "I've had a tough time answering that myself. The only way I can describe it, put my finger on it, is that I can see what's under the game face. I know him too well. That bullet did more than injure him. It knocked the stuffing out of him. I keep going back to everything I learned in all those years chasing degrees and that PhD in psychology. No matter the approach or methods that could help him, I only come up with one answer."

"Which is?"

"Time. He needs time to come to terms with what happened to him. Time to seek out whatever help he needs to do that. Time to talk it through and prioritize what is most important in his life. Time to decide where to go from here."

"As Prime Minister, he doesn't have the luxury of time," I said.

"I'm not sure any of us do."

I usually know how my wife thinks. But I wasn't prepared for that cryptic remark. "What do you mean, love?"

"The MP you sparred with today. Poirier. I can't prove it. But I think he could be what you called the bagman. The money link in the chain of guns, money, politics and the lunatic fringe. Remember the MP at the New Year's Eve party?"

"Apple Belly. Tried to corner me into commenting on banning handguns."

"He overheard Poirier making a deal for a large transfer of cash. For the cause, he said. MP Lockwood, aka Apple Belly, has been trying to pry more information out of Poirier for the prime minister. But so far, no luck."

"What does the PM think?"

"Poirier almost got kicked out of the Conservative Party caucus for violating campaign financing rules. My boss is halfway convinced Poirier's at it again. But Lockwood is sure the amount of money mentioned at that one meeting was over the million dollar mark."

"If that's just an installment …"

"Alec, I've told you this in confidence. So I've broken a confidence. As I said, I've got no proof."

"I wouldn't put anything past that dickhead." I held her closer and covered us in the puffed up comfort of the duvet. "If he's involved in any way with that network then there's got to be a way to prove it."

Chapter 48

Jerilynn

I got the call at seven the next morning. The Prime Minister would be released from hospital today to recuperate at Harrington Lake.

"Somehow I've got to keep this quiet."

"Keep what quiet?" My husband spit the foamy remains of toothpaste into the bathroom sink and wiped his mouth on a towel.

"Check out time for the prime minister is in two hours. The last thing he or his family needs is a flock of circling media."

"I'll call the commissioner, although she probably already knows. The RCMP detail will wrap around him and the limo they'll take him home in. I promise you nobody will get through."

After a quick shower, I slipped into the appropriate professional yet casual attire from my closet and applied a bit of makeup. The pile of papers that required the prime minister's attention and the RCMP incident report over-stuffed my sagging shoulder bag. I was out the door and on the road in thirty minutes, parked unnoticed behind the health care complex and breathed a sigh of relief. No media. Just a handful of people lined up along the sidewalk with a Canadian flag large enough to whip in the wind around the tallest pole.

The ripple of minor disturbance stirred by male voices echoed down the hallway and increased in volume the closer I got to the prime minister's hospital room. The door opened as I reached for the handle.

"Well, hello." Although we hadn't met, I knew the man with the lop-sided grin had to be Jonathan Reid. Celine had described the same sort of smile from her late husband that always brought a smile to her lips. I smiled at him. I couldn't help myself. The buoyancy of the prime minister's younger brother was contagious.

200

"Who are you?" Laugh lines under silvery grey eyes flecked with blue creased as his grin grew to a full blown smile. Equally tall and lean with a longer loose mop of auburn waves on his head, his obvious flirt oozed with the confidence of a man accustomed to attracting the opposite sex in copious numbers.

"Who is it, Jonathan dear?"

"I don't know, Mum. You tell me." He stepped aside to let me in.

"Jerilynn!" Celine came forward and gave me a quick hug.

"A beautiful name for a lovely lady."

Do you ever dial down the charm?

"For once in your life, could you please have some manners?" The prime minister stood in the middle of the room. His right hand gripped the handle of what I hoped was a locked wheelchair. He winced as Angeline slid the jacket sleeve up and over his left arm and injured shoulder.

"I'll be polite if you will. Introduce us."

"Jerilynn Connor is my chief of staff."

"Is that so? I've been here almost two weeks and I know I would have remembered seeing you," Jonathan said to me through the smile that never seemed to fade. "So why haven't I?"

"Timing," the prime minister said. "I made sure she was here when you were not."

A knock at the door and cheery request to enter broke up the barb fest between brothers. "Ready to go, Mr. Prime Minister?"

"Do I have to ride in this?" He frowned at the wheelchair. "I'd much prefer walking out on my own steam."

"Hospital rules, sir."

"How about he walks and you push me?" Jonathan's joke amused everyone but his brother.

"You two boys behave." Celine looped her arm through Jonathan's. "Evan, get in the chair."

If I hadn't seen and heard it, I wouldn't have believed the dynamics of the real life Reid family sitcom that played out from hospital departure to arrival at Harrington Lake.

True to his word, Alec had secured the RCMP blockade. Jonathan settled into the limo beside their mother and waved at the rows of men, women and children lining the streets and sidewalks with unfurled Canadian flags. The well-wishers applauded and waved back. The Prime Minister threatened to order the officers to leave his brother behind.

"I would have reconsidered my career options if I'd known about the perks of your job," Jonathan said to his brother. "Limousines, RCMP escorts, adoring crowds, a beautiful chief of staff." He lifted his chin and lop-sided grinned. "Go on. Thank me."

The smolder heated to simmer. Angeline saw and apparently sensed it, too. She reached for and lightly squeezed her husband's hand. "Evan. He's teasing you. Ignore it."

"I tell you what I'm going to do." The prime minister's dark eyes glared into his brother's. "As soon as I'm strong enough, I'm going to kick your ass." He leaned his head back into leather interior comfort and closed his eyes. "Then we'll go fishing."

"Have they always been like this?" I whispered in Celine's ear.

"Since they both learned to talk, my dear," she whispered back.

The Prime Minister did not join in the small talk banter or open his eyes during the half hour drive north to Gatineau. His only response was a nod when Angeline asked if he was OK. As I had no intention of getting out of the vehicle that would transport me back to my car, I emptied my bag and handed the pile of paperwork and incident report to an RCMP officer on our arrival at the lakefront main cottage. Angeline and Celine walked on ahead toward the lineup of Reid children anxious to greet the father they had not seen since he was nearly taken from them.

Jonathan reached in the limo door opened by a plainclothes officer in a suit. "I got this," he said.

"They're doing their job, Jon."

"So am I." Jonathan's arm circled his brother's waist. "This is why I'm here. Why I've always been here."

I watched them walk together, slowly and with care. Evan leaned into and accepted the strength he needed. His daughters hugged him. His son opened the door for him. His family welcomed him home.

Chapter 49

Evan

Pain management comes at a cost. Take the drug and the body functions better but the mind loses its edge. The brain demands sleep. Rest and the pain eventually returns. I take more to move the injured parts in relative comfort. My mind dulls. I close my eyes. I sleep.

The checklist of 'still can't do that' got longer with my release from hospital. The days lost to this continuous loop of frustration and debilitation flowed from morning to night without purpose or recollection. My precious family's lives went on around and mostly without me. I read but could not fully comprehend the words on the official papers of government that Jerilynn had brought with her and left for my attention.

My country would have to wait for me. But I was confident that Canada was safe in the highly competent hands of my cabinet.

"You can totally have this job." Carla Mendez, the current occupant of the hot seat until my return, flipped through the pile of paper closest to her with the nudge of a worn eraser at the end of a well-chewed pencil. Sorted piles stacked on the long low table in front of the best lake view seats in the retreat house reminded me of my classroom desk the week before the start of school.

"Ah! Here's what I've been looking for," she said.

The automatic reach with my left hand fired nerves and tissue not yet healed. With no pain meds to dull the stab, I grit my teeth and endured.

"Are you all right?" Carla's concern overshadowed the business at hand. Her quick glances searched the room for help and backup. "Do you need me to …"

"No. I'm fine."

"I can take care of the rest of this."

"I know you can. That's why I recruited you away from the peace and serenity of Vancouver."

"About that." She put the pencil down and shifted position on the cushion. Her expression communicated a mixed blend of emotion. "I told you going into this that I would only stay as long as you did."

I tried for brevity. What came out bordered on rude. "Sorry I couldn't give you a heads-up. An assassination attempt wasn't on that day's itinerary."

"That's not what I meant."

"I know and I don't know why I said that. I'm sorry, Carla."

"There's no apology necessary. If I'd been through what you have, I'd be a helluva lot less cordial." She shuffled the sorted piles into stacks more manageable for transport. "Have you decided what you're going to tell the party? You did promise me a heads-up on that."

"No, I haven't and I have my reasons."

"Well, those reasons must be very important to you. In my humble opinion, you've given more than enough to party and country. If I were you, I'd tell them to find someone else."

"And that's not going to be you, is it?"

"Not a chance." She made a sweeping gesture over the stacks with her hand. "This has soured me on staying in government at all. I can't wait to get back to the mostly paperless world of digital media marketing." She packed up the paperwork. "Third reading of the gun ban bill amendment is three weeks from today. I can take care of that if you need me to."

"I will be there for third reading even if I have to defy doctor's orders."

"Ah." She shook her finger at me. "There's the reason." She stood to leave before I could deny or confirm that truth. "Don't get up. I can see myself out. Promise me you'll take all the time you need to take care of yourself."

"I promise."

§

A day of denying debilitation had taken its toll. Mum saw through my lame excuse to skip family dinner, filled a plate and followed me to the bedroom she'd shared with Dad when he was prime minister. The cluck of her tongue as she fluffed my pillow and tucked me into bed transported me back in time to the boy I once was here when my greatest personal challenge was catching a bigger fish than Jon's. Mum handed me a fork and stayed until I'd swallowed every bite of beef, mushrooms and noodles. She took the dish away and returned with a glass of water and the bottle of pain meds.

"You'll always be my beautiful boy," she said and kissed my fore-head. I fell asleep to the soft click of the door closing behind her. I woke when Angeline turned back the sheet and duvet on her side of the bed and lay down beside me.

She reached for my hand and laced her fingers through mine. "How are you feeling, love?" she asked.

"Sore and tired. But I can't complain. You're here and so am I." Her sob startled me. "Oh, Angeline. Love. Please don't. I didn't mean to … "

"I haven't. I couldn't." The steady flow of her tears contrasted with uneven intake of breaths between words and phrases. "I had to be strong. For you. For your Mum. For the children. Even Jon."

I held her. Stroked her hair. Whispered my love for her as the delayed pent up emotional pain poured out of her.

"He was frantic to get on that plane. Relieved that when he got here you were awake and talking to us. Celine had gone back to Rideau Cottage to rest and be with our children. But he insisted that my place was with them. He slept in a chair next to your bed. Did you know he was there?"

"Yeah. He snored."

Her laughter helped stop the tears. The calm of quiet in a retreat surrounded by nature and a household deep in slumber settled us in the surety that nothing could harm us here in the peace of this moment.

"How are the children?" I asked her.

"Can't you tell?"

"I'm not sure. It's like they're afraid that I'm not really here. That they'll wake up in the morning and I'll be gone and I won't be back."

"What you're really asking is how they were while you were gone."

"I guess I am."

Angeline snuggled up against my uninjured side. "Celine and I had already gone to hospital when the RCMP brought the children home that day. Isaac told me Gabrielle went to her bedroom and slammed the door. She cried most of the night, he said. She refused to come out of her room for dinner or even to have a piece of her birthday cake."

I groaned. I'd forgotten the day I might have died was the beginning of my daughter's fourteenth year of life. "She didn't have the party she'd been looking forward to. We've got to make that up to her."

"Yes, we do. She and I have talked about that. She doesn't want a party with her friends. Only family for now. She insisted. I was surprised at that but then the more I thought about it I wasn't at all."

"What did she say that changed your mind?"

"It wasn't what she said but what she didn't say. I think Gabrielle suffered the most because she's old enough to understand what did and could have happened. Isaac didn't cry or ask me anything. He took on the responsibility and did his best to be the man of the house. He did chores without being asked. Helped Corina with her homework and carried her back pack without complaint. Stopped calling his sister 'Gabby Grumpy Pants'."

I grinned at that revelation. "What about my *mon petit ange?*"

"She cried every night at bedtime. But she never gave up hope. Every morning at breakfast she'd say 'Daddy will be home soon.'"

That's when the anger boiled up. Who had done this to me and my family? And why? I'd read and re-read the incident report prepared for the commission. I'd searched for that answer and not found it.

I knew who would have it.

208

Chapter 49

Alec

Jerilynn answered her cell phone and handed it to me.

"What's up?"

"The prime minister wants to talk to you."

I dropped the spoon into my empty cereal bowl. "Good morning, Prime Minister."

"You know the rule when I'm at Harrington Lake, Alec."

"Yes, but when I'm in uniform I follow my own."

"Fair enough. I have questions about the commission's incident report, which was excellent, by the way. Very thorough."

"Apparently not thorough enough or you wouldn't have questions. Ask away."

"I'd prefer to meet in person and return a favor. Would you and Jerilynn be available to have dinner with us here tomorrow evening? No strings attached. Lord knows there are more than enough cooks in this kitchen at the moment."

"Give me a minute to confer with the management."

He laughed. "Of course."

"What?" J-lynn asked.

"We've been invited to another Reid family dinner. Tomorrow."

"Love to."

"I heard that," he said. "I'd like to talk with you before dinner which I'm told will be served at seven."

"We'll be there by six."

Jerilynn slid her phone in her jacket pocket. "So are you going to tell me what that was all about?"

"Incident report review."

"It looked complete to me. I wonder what else he wants to know."

I stacked our breakfast dishes in the dishwasher and helped myself to our usual 'there's more where this came from' morning kiss. "I guess I'll find out tomorrow."

If I were in his shoes, I know what I'd ask.

Chapter 50

Evan

I remembered reading a passage from a book as an undergrad student in philosophy class. A man was lowered deep into a mine shaft where the darkness was palpable and the cold chilled him until his bones ached. The hard packed earth jolted him at rock bottom. When he was pulled back up and asked what he found, he said darkness, cold and dirt. We knew that, they said. But where are the diamonds? A person can't begin to heal until the darkness and the cold are forgotten, the dirt washes away and all that remains are the diamonds.

My three bright diamonds were due home from school. Healing begins at home.

"Daddy!" Corina ran through the open front door. Her arms reached up to me. My heart hurt more than my shoulder would if I tried to pick her up.

"I'm sorry, *mon petit ange*," I said. "I can't do that yet."

"That's OK, Daddy." She patted the couch cushion. "You sit here. I'll be right back." She skipped away as Isaac wandered in dragging a pair of back packs, his and the other stamped with a sparkly pink fairy princess.

"Hi Dad," he said. No complaints about carrying the extra burden. He let go of the straps and turned toward the kitchen.

"Where are you going, little man?" I asked him.

"To take out the garbage and see if Mom needs help."

"Come here first. I want to talk to you."

"OK." He sat on the cushion next to mine.

"Thank you for taking care of things while I was in hospital."

He shrugged and folded his hands in his lap. "It was no big deal."

"Yes, it was. And it's great that you're still helping out. I really appreciate that."

"I, uh .. "

"What do you want to say to me, Isaac? *Dit-le-moi, s'il te plaît.*" Please tell me.

His shoulders sagged. His hands gripped jeans-covered knees. "I did it so I wouldn't think about it because I was scared. I didn't want to be a grown up yet. I wanted you to come back!" He sucked in his bottom lip, buried his head in my lap, and began to cry in great gulping howling sobs as little boys do.

I rubbed and patted his back as I had to relieve the ache in his tummy during those long ago nights of relentless colic. Corina returned with a fleece blanket from her dolly's bed and her favored stuffed purple llama. She tucked the blanket around my healing shoulder. "We'll take care of you, Daddy," she said and squirmed up alongside me. The llama's nose touched my cheek.

After dinner, my third diamond plopped The Complete Works of William Shakespeare on the table cleared of dishes. Gabrielle dragged a chair away from the table and sat down hard. "*C'est ridicule!*" she grumbled and flipped the book open to a bookmarked page.

"What's ridiculous?" I asked.

"This!"

"Much Ado About Nothing, Act 5, Scene 2," I read aloud. "What's the assignment?"

"The theme of this ridiculously long play is apparently somewhere in this scene. I'm supposed to find it and explain why I think that is the theme."

"I see."

"I've read it a gazillion times and I can't see it! *C'est ridicule*!"

"Do you want my help?"

"Yes! Please, Dad. The assignment is due tomorrow."

"Alright. Let's go through it." The pain meds were beginning to wear off. Good because I could think more clearly. Bad because when the ache got worse I couldn't think at all. I positioned myself in the chair and hoped chemically-induced comfort would last a bit longer. "Who are Benedick and Beatrice? What is their relationship?"

"He loves her but she doesn't want anything to do with him. He seems like a nice guy but she's not so nice. I don't know what he sees in her."

"Why is that?"

"She's mean to him."

"Is she mean only to him?"

"She's the most mean to him. But she's just not a nice person. She doesn't seem happy."

"Does she tell him why she's not happy?"

"Not in so many words." Gabrielle leaned closer to the text. "Maybe she's sick. She does say she's very ill."

"Read it to me."

"Well, he says 'and now tell me, how doth your cousin?' And she says 'Very ill.' And he says 'And how do you?' And she replies 'very ill, too.' Maybe that has a double meaning?"

"What do you think?"

"I think so. Maybe her cousin is physically sick. But Beatrice is saying she's sick in another way. Mentally or emotionally. So is she asking him to help her get better?"

"Read the next line. What does Benedick say?"

"Serve God, love me, and mend." Gabrielle seemed to ponder the answer as she focused on the mist of twilight distorting the trees' shadows beyond the windows. "That's it, isn't it?" She looked to me for confirmation. "That's the theme."

Our love made this child. Beautiful and strong like her mother. Searching for wisdom and pursuing the answers as I have always done. "*Oui, ma fille chérie.*" Yes, my darling daughter.

Her bottom lip quivered. She blinked back the tears that dampened her eyelashes. "*Je t'aime papa.*" She closed the book, kissed my cheek, and left for her place of solitude with the collected works of The Bard.

Chapter 51

Alec

Had I acted on my gut reaction to the guy who opened the front door at Harrington Lake, he would never father children.

"Well hello again, Jerilynn. Memory doesn't do your beauty the justice it deserves."

There's some shit talk to shovel. Whoever this dickhead was, he resembled the man I was here to see. Eyes on me, not on her, buddy!

"Alec, this is Evan's brother Jonathan." My wife sideways spooned herself to me with one hand at the small of my back and the other on my chest. I almost laughed at her uncharacteristic adoring puppy-love look up at me. "Jonathan, this is my husband RCMP Chief Superintendent Alec Martin."

Her act had no effect on him. He didn't miss a beat or drop the smile. "Only our Mum calls me Jonathan. I'm Jon." He stuck out his hand. Same impressive grip as Evan. "Please come in. Make yourselves at home."

The Reid family greeting continued along and into the main living areas of the PM's summer residence and retreat. Celine and Angeline said hello, hugged J-lynn and spirited her away toward the kitchen. Corina bounded past the women and tugged on my shirt sleeve. "Are you gonna make macaroni and cheese?"

"Not this time," I said. "But I did give your Mom my recipe." The pure and unconditional exuberance for life in every movement, word and smile from this little girl heightened my hope and desire for J-lynn and I to start our family soon. I was so ready to be Dad.

Her crinkled nose temporarily erased a sprinkle of freckles. "Mommy's wasn't as good as yours."

"Neither was the spaghetti." Isaac swiveled around in an overstuffed chair nearer the fireplace. An earbud attached to the boy's listening device of choice dangled at his left cheek.

"Hey, guys." Jon clapped and rubbed his hands together. "I could use some help setting the table for dinner."

"I'll help!" Corina scampered to the kitchen. Isaac swiveled back around in the chair.

"Well, that wasn't an entirely successful diversion," Jon said. "I'll be right there, sweetheart," he called to Corina. "My brother is waiting for you in his office," he said to me.

I followed him to an open door at the opposite end of the cottage. Evan was sitting at an L-shaped unit with its backs against walls beneath windows that framed more breath-taking views of nature. The incident report lay open on the desk to the page with bullet trajectory charts and graphs.

"Alec. Come in."

He'd lost some weight. The paler pallor of his skin was to be expected due to the severity of the trauma he'd experienced. I tried to block memory recall of the last time I'd seen him. Unconscious on a gurney. Being wheeled out and lifted into the back of an ambulance. "How are you, Evan?"

He closed the report. "On the right side of the grass and grateful to be here."

I had the eerie sensation that he'd somehow read my mind.

"Please. Have a seat," he said.

"Can I get anyone a beer?" Jon asked.

"I'm good for now, thanks," I said.

"I'll pass until after dinner," Evan replied.

"OK, then I'll leave you to do business." Jon turned on his heel and left us alone.

"So." I got right down to it. "What questions do you have about the report?"

He didn't waste time, either. "Willie Carlyle, the night security guard who tried to kill me. Jerilynn said she knew him, or at least knew of him. She told me he froze his hands starting her car in The Hill parking lot last December."

"That sounds about right."

"Did you talk to him? Interrogate him?"

"More like interview him with counsel present since he pled guilty. But yes, I did."

"He wasn't involved in this hate crime network described in the report."

"He was not."

Evan leaned forward in the chair. "If his motive wasn't political or an attempt to stop the gun ban bill amendment vote, then why did he want me dead?"

There it was, the why that had baffled me. The motive I'd extrapolated from Willie's statement. The answer I'd arrived at and was prepared to give. "To bring peace to his family."

His reaction was not what I expected. I'd braced for anger or confusion. But not calm. "Tell me what he told you," he said.

As I relayed the sad saga of the tortured Carlyle family, the usual darkness of his eyes softened and faded. "In his mind, Willie thought if the living embodiment of his father's bitterness were no longer living, William Carlyle's reason to hate would be gone. His sister and niece would move back in with his mother and her reasons for living would not leave her behind and alone with his abusive father."

Muffled sounds of family drifted down the hallway. Voices. Laughter. Corina's cry of "that's not fair!"

Evan rubbed his eyes. "There but for the grace of God." He sat back in the chair. "The irony of this is not lost on me. The Carlyle's story could have been mine."

"I think that's a bit of a stretch." I didn't tell him a similar analogy had crossed my mind.

"Is it? Poor guy just wanted some kind of normal. What he got was anything but. I can relate to that. Politics churns out casualties. I came close to being another because of a man and his family that already were."

"Dinner is on the table." Angeline leaned in from the hallway, her hand on the office door frame. "Are you two at a stopping point?"

The presence of his wife shifted Evan's mood from melancholy empathy to love and outright adoration. "Yes, my love. We'll be right there."

That's when I got angry for him, for Angeline and their children. For J-lynn and me and the family we hoped to have. No matter the motive, Willie Carlyle had no right to end his father's vendetta of hate through a violent act that could have taken irreplaceable lives from us. The handgun he'd used had been stolen from its legal owner. Evan was right. The only way to prevent such tragedies was to make handgun ownership illegal.

§

After dinner and a beer with the Reid brothers, my wife drove us home. She wasn't at all impaired by alcohol. I noticed she'd passed on wine at dinner and asked for a glass of water.

"You seemed to be getting along with Jon."

"What made you say that?"

"Well, you two did get off to a rocky start." Her sideways glance and grin hinted at sarcasm. "Were you jealous or being overly possessive?"

"A bit of both." I reached over and squeezed her thigh. "He's not such a bad guy. Just way too full of himself."

"That he is. So, did you have the answers for whatever it was my boss wanted to know?"

"Yes, but I sure wasn't prepared for the response."

"How do you mean?"

"He felt sorry for the guy who tried to kill him. If you hadn't been there, I have little doubt that he would have succeeded. Your boss is a better man than I am. If I were Evan, I'd be in the House of Commons arguing to reinstate the death penalty."

"You're sure about that."

"Hell, yes."

I cringed at the scrape of tires along the curb in front of our townhouse. Parallel parking was a skill my wife had yet to master.

"You never know how you will act or react to a situation until you're faced with it." Her halo of white blonde hair glowed in street light reflected through the windshield. "I know we've talked about starting a family. But talking about it and the reality of it is totally different."

The spark of hope for fatherhood flickered. "Honey." I smoothed back loose wispy strands from her halo. "Do you have something to tell me?"

"I think I'm pregnant."

So that's why she'd passed on the chardonnay! My smile was wider than Corina's when she'd asked if I was going to make macaroni and cheese.

Chapter 52

Evan

Fishing rods, cans of insect repellant and Mum's warning to clean whatever we caught wherever we docked the boat traditionally marked the first long weekend of our summers as the sons of Tony Reid. The best I could manage this year was a beer with my brother in Adirondack chairs anchored on the lakeshore.

The spirit on that clear blue sky Victoria Day morning envisioned me dressed in layers to peel off when the air heated by sunlight lifted with the mist and lingering chill over water cold as melted ice. In my mind's eye, waves rippled from the easy skim of the boat to the spots where Jon, the loons and I would search the clear depths for trout. Bait on hooks at the end of our rods lured what the lake had for us to take. The hours spun out like fishing line measured in timeless moments spent doing nothing together but waiting for the fish to bite.

My spirit cursed the flesh that was still too weak.

"Cut yourself some slack, man." Jon reached into the opened cooler between our chairs and pulled out two bottles. Foam oozed up and over the necks with the hiss and click of the top bent by the opener and popped from the glass. "You've been out of hospital less than a month." He handed mine over and took a long pull on his.

"How many nights did you sleep in that chair next to my bed?" I asked.

"You mean that too short lumpy hospital issue recliner?" He rubbed his neck. "I don't know. At least three. Maybe five nights. I know my knees and shoulders will never be the same."

"I don't know if my shoulder will ever come back."

"What do the doc and the physiotherapist say?"

"The surgeon thinks it will. The physiotherapist says it could take six months."

"Well, that sucks. But, hey," he touched the neck of his bottle to mine, "you're still here."

"For that I am beyond grateful. I've said that every day since. I should have said this sooner. I am glad you made the trip. Mum really needed you to be here."

"So did you. And so did I." He finished his beer and opened another.

"Really."

Dad admired Jon for his natural ability to rein in his emotions from an early age. "Watch and learn," he'd say. "Be more like your brother." Jon would laugh at my outbursts which of course only escalated my outrage. I'd never seen Jon even close to angry. Until now.

"What are you trying to say?" He slapped his open palm on the armrest of the wooden chair. "That I don't care? Hell yes, I care! I was in a panic to get the first flight out I could! I must have come up with a thousand ways to kill that son of a bitch with the gun while that bird was in the air between Christchurch and Ottawa. I was scared shitless that I'd get here too late."

He leaned back in the chair in much the same way as I do to cool down and regain control. "No matter what you think of me and my life choices, or lack of them, I love you and I will always be there for you. Like I said the day you were released from hospital and needed a hand getting out of that limo, that's my job. We're family."

Admit it, I thought. *We're brothers. Say what has and always will be there.*

Mid-afternoon rays of sunlight on the lake reflected in ribbons of glare and shadow. Waves lapped the boat dock and boat tied to it that we had launched from and rowed as three and then two. Jon would be leaving next week. I wanted him to stay. "So, how long are planning to be in New Zealand?"

"Awhile longer. I bought a bar."

I nearly choked on my beer. "You did what now?"

"You heard me."

"When did this happen?"

"A week ago Tuesday."

I groaned and dropped my empty bottle in the cooler. "Jesus, Jon."

"I'm kidding. Actually, it's more of a bar and restaurant. I bought into the business about six months ago at the start of summer season."

"What the hell do you know about running a bar and restaurant?"

"I know enough. I love to eat and I love to drink."

"Those are unique qualifications."

"Relax. I have a business partner. She just got divorced from a wealthy guy, cleaned his clock and had money to invest. But I digress. Tamara was a chef on a cruise ship, managed a bar in Wellington and earned her chops working with her dad at his restaurant in Auckland. She's the real deal. So far, business has been good, better than we expected. Hey, I'm happy with my life. Are you?"

"My personal life, yeah, I couldn't be happier. But I had to take a bullet to spend quality time with my family. And while we're on that subject, in case you hadn't noticed a Canadian I promised to keep safe tried to assassinate me. Angeline was inches away from being a widow and my kids without their father."

"That freaked you out."

"Wouldn't you be?"

"Yes, I guess I would. But that's not all that's bothering you. So out with it."

I stifled a laugh and shook my head. "I never could keep a secret from you."

"Comes with the sibling territory. I know what you're going to say before you do." Jon opened and handed me another beer.

"Before this happened Angeline threatened to leave me. She'd had enough of being a single parent."

"That was an empty threat. Angeline would never leave you. She adores you."

"I know that. And I worship the ground she walks on. She and the kids are my life. And I've missed so much of that life."

"Well, you can do something about that. The writ drops in a few weeks. The election is less than five months away. Odds are the Liberals will win again. Are you going to keep leading your party? Or put Parliament Hill in the rearview mirror? What are you going to do, Mr. Prime Minister?"

"I don't know yet."

"Yeah, you do." We took time out from talking to listen and be in the moment. Here at a place we'd known and might not have again. Jon leaned toward me over the thick and wide wooden arm of the Adirondack chair. "We'll all accept and live with whatever you decide. All we ask is that you're sure you can live with the reasons for that decision."

What I decide depends on Wednesday's vote for reasons only Jerilynn knows. "I've been on The Hill fourteen years, six years as a back-bencher and eight years in the hot seat. This might be the right time to get out of that chair and let somebody else sit in it."

"Maybe so. Any ideas on what's next?"

"I could go back to teaching."

"Or you could move to Christchurch and work at my bar."

Somehow I managed to keep a straight face despite the comical mental images of me mixing the wrong drinks and mopping up epic spills with bar rags. "Thanks for the offer but I don't think so," I said. "I'm not sure I could get used to summer in December."

"Yeah, it's an adjustment for sure. Besides, my business couldn't afford to absorb the wasted liquor costs."

That did it. Two beers and a shared joke unleashed desperately needed belly laughs between brothers. When I recovered, I said what needed saying straight from the heart. "I love you, too."

Chapter 53

Jerilynn

The fresh-brewed coffee in my cup smelled like skunk. One whiff and my stomach threatened to expel what wasn't in it. Tomorrow's appointment with the OB-GYN would no doubt confirm what I already knew without the blue lines on the pregnancy test strip.

Keep your mind on today, Jerilynn. Sending the handgun ban bill amendment on to the Senate and royal assent depended on it. In his absence, the prime minister was relying on me to fulfill a personal promise entrusted in confidence. Deputy Prime Minister Carla Mendez needed all my help to prepare for what could be a long and difficult debate in the House of Commons.

My cell phone lit up as the printer spit out the final paper for the amendment debate file.

"How are you feeling, honey?" Alec had pressed a cool cloth to my forehead and rubbed my back as I'd knelt at the porcelain throne that morning.

"I can't drink coffee or anything else for that matter. I'm fine as long as I don't think about it. What's up?"

"Your boss is on the way."

"I'm ready for her."

"Not her. Him."

"What?!"

"I just got the word from the prime minister's detail."

"Wow. Well, this puts a new last minute spin on things. Thanks for the heads-up, love."

I flipped through the paperwork. Everything was in order but for one glaring omission. The prepared speech, the most vital element, had been written for the deputy prime minister to deliver. The bell would summon Parliamentarians in one hour. The prime minister strolled through his office door twenty minutes after Alec's call.

My response was not appropriate. I stood in the middle of the room, hands on my hips and a frown on my face. "What are you doing here?" I said.

His response was not what I expected. He laughed! "I know I haven't been here for a while. But this is my office." He walked around his desk and sat behind it. "We don't have much time. What have you got for me?"

I picked up the pile of paper in the file and lay it in front of him. Outward signs of the reason for his absence showed in the looser fit of the dark blue suit he wore and the obvious limited use of his left arm. "Are you sure that you're ready for this?" I asked.

He skimmed the pages in the file and reached in the pocket of his jacket. "I have to be. It's now or never. Suck it up, Evan. You're Tony Reid's son." He handed me a jump drive. "Print out what's on here for me, please."

"With all due respect, your father was not shot by a would-be assassin."

He leaned back in the chair and nodded, his eyebrows raised. "You're right. He wasn't. I am the first Right Honourable Prime Minister who can lay claim to that dubious distinction. When this amendment passes and the bill becomes law, I hope to be the last."

The jump drive had only one file. I didn't read what rolled out of the printer.

He glanced at the paper I handed him and added it to the top of the stack in the folder. "Walk with me." His movements were slower but with a deliberate feel and air of confidence that he would and could take on any opponent. He stopped in mid-stride at the office door and turned back to me. "By the way, it has come to my attention that you committed another serious breach of protocol."

How could he have found out about the phone call from Margot? I knew Alec would never break that confidentiality. Margot certainly wouldn't. As far as I knew, no one else had been privy to that conversation.

"You called me by name outside the House of Commons."

Relief released the butterflies from my already churning stomach. I clicked through my memory in search of the moment when I might have been guilty of this transgression and realized what he meant. As I'd begged for his life that horrible afternoon, I'd cried out my fear of losing him. *Evan! Please. Breathe!*

"Yes, Prime Minister."

The dark color in his eyes had faded. His smile was warm and genuine. He kissed my cheek and spoke our words of endearment, a secret pact of friendship for my ear alone. "*Merci, mon amie.* Thank you for saving my life."

We walked together to the opened door at the House of Commons. I turned back at the spot where he had fallen just five weeks before.

Chapter 54

Evan

I crossed the threshold of the familiar, a stranger where everything had changed.

An undercurrent shuffle of soles and heels on shoes, papers in folders, muffled cleared throats and coughs settled to silence after the bell. MPs on my side of the aisle stood and applauded as I entered. Respectful nods and hands extended for me to shake lined the path to my place behind the bench. The Speaker called the House to order.

"Mr. Speaker."

"The Right Honourable Prime Minister."

I didn't open the folder in front of me. Words chosen and written by the prime minister were not what Evan Reid had to say.

"I stand before you a victim and survivor of violence carried out by a person with a handgun. No one should feel the excruciating pain and debilitation of a bullet deliberately fired into their body as I did. No family should fear the loss of a loved one to a senseless act of hate as did my wife, my mother, my brother and my children. To me and for them, this is no longer a political issue or policy decision. It's personal. Mr. Speaker, I implore the Honourable Members of Parliament as a husband, a son, a brother, a father and a Canadian. Make the amendment to this bill law. Do what you can – what you must – to keep us all safe."

I sat down, folded my hands in my lap, and waited for the response.

"Mr. Speaker."

"The Member from Lethbridge."

Margot Isley, the retired doctor who had used her scarf to staunch the hemorrhage from the hole in my shoulder, stood up from her seat in the Conservative Party back bench. "I move the amendment to Bill C-71 banning the private sale and ownership of handguns be approved as presented on third reading."

House leader Asad Bashir rose with the grumble across the aisle from opposition MPs displeased that one of their own would support Liberal Party legislation without debate. "Mr. Speaker."

"The Member from Outremont."

"I second the motion."

Three hundred sixteen Members of Parliament voted in favor. Politicians representing five parties and independents got to their feet and applauded their decision. The twenty Tories and two members of the Bloc Quebecois that did not remained seated. As did I until the Speaker adjourned the session.

I expended the strength conserved for debate greeting well-wishers and opponents that graciously accepted defeat for the sake of all Canadians.

"Testifying from firsthand experience is one way to get a bill passed." Carla Mendez walked back with me to my office. "Extreme. But nevertheless effective."

"Yeah, I wouldn't recommend it." I sat down hard in the chair behind my desk and thanked Jerilynn for the glass of water she brought me.

"So, now that the bill amendment you stayed to pass is on a likely fast track through Senate approval and royal assent, have you made a decision on what you'll tell the party?" Carla asked.

"I'm about ninety-eight percent there." The glass in my hand was sweating almost as much as I was. My hand trembled with the effort required to drink. Cool water going down helped revive me. "I need a few days to wrap my head around what just happened."

"OK. I'll give you that. But I'm holding you to that promise."

"I'll let you know ahead of caucus."

"That's all I ask." She leaned across my desk and shook my hand. "Congratulations, Prime Minister. You accomplished what you came to do."

"Get his detail to take him home," I heard her say on her way out. As always, Jerilynn was way ahead of her.

"The RCMP is ready when you are."

I drank the rest of the water in the glass and waved my chief of staff in. She sat in the chair I'd brought in to interview her almost eight years ago. We'd gone the distance together. Through budget battles, provincial skirmishes with premiers and MPs threatening succession, a pandemic that rocked our country's core and took too many from us. All the while fighting to keep Canadians safe without knowing that she and I were not.

"You're the only one who knows why I had to be here for third reading. Why this fight was so important to me."

She nodded acknowledgement of a privileged confidentiality shared. "I'm glad you were able to keep your personal promise to Keme. You know your secret will always be safe with me."

"Can I ask you to do me a favor?"

"Of course."

"Now that the vote is over, would you pick out a scarf for your friend MP, uh, Margot? A thank you gift. Not necessarily from me."

Jerilynn grinned and winked. "I gotcha. Sure, I can do that." She got up when my detail arrived.

"Now go home and stay there until all your stuffing is back where it belongs."

She left my office before I could ask what she meant.

Hours later, after family dinner and a birthday cake with thirteen candles, Angeline lay in my arms. I closed my eyes. Breathed her in and with her. Thankful to be alive and to be loved by and make love to the most beautiful woman I would ever know.

"I'm so proud of you, my love. You've accomplished so much. Done so much for so many."

I considered her words and mine before I spoke. I wanted to be clear for both of us. "The victory today wasn't nearly as sweet as I thought it would be. The cost was nearly too high. I've lost count of how many times in the last eight years that I've regretted saying yes to the Liberal Party. Wished that I would have said no to my father and my brother six years before that. Thought I should have stayed a teacher."

"But you did, my love. You are a teacher. You've taught us all what it means to be kind and caring and willing to do whatever it takes when you believe it's the right thing to do. You've shown our country and the world what it truly means to be a leader."

I opened my eyes and saw the love in hers, warm and blue as a mid-summer sky.

"I know what I said before this happened. And now I have another very good reason to stand my ground and insist that eight years is enough. But whatever you decide I will be with you at your side where I've always been, where I will always be. Our children, our family, will stay together with you wherever that may be. I could never leave you, Evan. I love you. That's forever and always."

I kissed her, deeply and passionately, grateful in the certainty of us. "I don't deserve you."

She snuggled closer and sighed. "Nonsense."

I heard my father's voice in that moment, insisting that I learn to ride a bicycle without training wheels to hold me up. He was right. Training wheels wouldn't have kept me from riding in front of that car. I did that all on my own. At any point along the timeline of my life, I had been free to make choices that would have changed everything. The help I had along the way brought me to this moment. My father repaired my broken bicycle and insisted that I get back on it. That lesson carried me through every challenge on Parliament Hill. My mother encouraged me to follow my heart to the front of a classroom and my brother found the soul mate who would own my heart for life. My son and daughters showed me how to feel the pure joy and wonder of seeing a fledgling robin fly for the first time or read their first words aloud. Jerilynn, my brilliant, relentlessly loyal chief of staff and friend had risked her life to save mine. My Angeline celebrated the wins, suffered the losses and sent me strength when she was running near empty. To have turned and walked away at any point would have erased it all.

I had made the right choices then. I knew what I had to do now.

Chapter 55

Jerilynn

It seemed like a different lifetime when he'd first held my hand and walked me home from Liverpool Regional High School. In the reality of this lifetime, the father of our child laced his fingers through mine, pumped his fist and yelped with joy.

"Well, I'm glad that you're happy." I felt a bit embarrassed at the smiles, nods and uttered congratulations from other patients waiting to see the doctor. "I'm just surprised at how happy."

"Honey," my husband said as we walked the hall to the clinic's front door. "I would have been happy with a house full of kids."

"Why didn't you say anything?"

"Because, love of my life, it's your body, your career and your choice. I wouldn't try to talk you into something you weren't ready for." He stopped at the curb where our car was parked. "You are ready for this." He turned me toward him with his hands on my shoulders. The concern that had chased away his glee was so genuine I didn't know whether to laugh or cry. "Are you ready for this? Be honest."

I reached up, touched his cheek and rose up on my toes for the follow-up kiss. "I've been ready since we said 'I do'."

His concern transitioned to confusion. "We only just started talking seriously about getting pregnant three months ago."

"I've always been sure about having a family just not so sure about the timing. Then, I thought maybe I'd waited too long."

"What do you mean by waited too long?"

I opened the passenger side car door. "A public sidewalk isn't the place to talk about this." I got in the car.

"Apparently not." He closed my door, rounded the trunk and settled in under the steering wheel. "But I'm not going to wait until we get home." He turned the key in the ignition and steered the car into heavy end-of-workday traffic.

"That's fine as long as you don't get distracted and run a red light or the car into a pole."

"I'm a cop. I can multi-task. And don't change the subject." Alec applied the brakes and waved a pair of pedestrians through the crossing in the road marked by white stripes. "Why did you think we waited too long? You're only thirty-four. Women have waited longer than that to start a family."

"I haven't had a shot in over a year."

Alec made a sharp right turn into a parking lot, slotted the car into an empty space and silenced the engine with the turn of his key. "Exactly when were you planning to share that piece of information?"

"I just did."

"Don't play games."

When he wouldn't look at me, I started to worry. And talk. "We weren't ready when we got married. We both knew that. Then our jobs got more complicated. I missed appointments and nothing happened. I'd reschedule, go in, get the shot and miss another appointment three months later. I took the pill during the pandemic. I think I got another shot when I went in for the vaccine. Then I just stopped doing anything. And still nothing happened."

"Why didn't you tell me?"

"I was afraid to find out if anything would ever happen whether I was on birth control or not. Was it a physical problem that I couldn't conceive? Emotional? Stress? I didn't want either of us to feel guilty about whatever the problem was or, heaven forbid, blame the other. That's just too toxic." He stared through the windshield at shoppers rolling metal baskets to open trunks and car doors. *Say something, Alec!* I screamed in my head.

"Well, whatever it was isn't a factor anymore." He reached over and again laced his fingers in mine. "So what was it? What changed?"

"I was going to reschedule and get another shot because I wasn't sure if you were ready. Then we had dinner with the Reid family." I stroked his arm with my fingertips. "I watched you with Evan and Angeline's children. Saw how you were with them, especially Corina. That's when I knew you were ready."

His soft, sweet kiss and whispered 'I love you' calmed my nerves and ended the worry. "Remind me to thank them for inviting us to dinner," he said.

We joked and laughed like a couple of high school kids the rest of the way home. Later that night as the full moon blocked out all but the brightest stars that twinkled through the skylight above our bed, I teased Alec about his tender yet tentative attempts at love-making. "I've been pregnant for ten weeks, love. I won't shatter and I'm damn sure not going to push you away."

"Oh my God." His caress and fondle abruptly stopped. "Ten weeks." He held me close. "I could have lost you both."

I shivered at the chilling implication of what he meant. Three lives might have been taken that day in the flash of a bullet fired from a handgun.

"Don't think about that. You didn't. I'm here." I took his hand and pressed his palm to me over the place within where our child would grow. "We're here."

Chapter 56

June ~The Caucus

The opposition party benefactor opened his opulent private study through a garden door partially obscured by the sweetly fragrant showy white blooms and abundant green of climbing hydrangea. Stale air within the cathedral beamed high-ceilinged sanctuary smelled of leather bound books, second-hand Cuban cigar smoke, and furniture polish. Velvet drapes drawn over tall and narrow leaded windows blocked out first-day-of-summer sunlight.

Four men gathered around a knee-level oval table carved and constructed from finely-textured ebony wood imported from Equatorial West Africa. Ornate chairs with padded seats covered by maroon velvet duplicated materials in the table and draperies. Pocket doors that separated the restricted entry bastion of solitude from the family's residence parted. A uniformed domestic employed by the host stepped silently over plush carpet. Four squat-stemmed snifters and a long-necked crystal decanter of spirits aged in the southwest region of France moved from the gold-rimmed glass tray in the server's hand to the mirror finish of the table.

The meeting at an exclusive by invitation only time and place was called to unofficial order, near yet a world away from Parliament Hill. The convener poured and swirled cognac in the snifter that rested between thick fingers in the fleshy pads of his palm. He loosened and removed his tie and opened the collar of his starched white dress shirt. "Well gentlemen. It appears the Tories will be unceremoniously handed our heads and squarely kicked in the backside by the Liberals come October."

"There is no effective political strategy that will defeat a surviving martyr." The dark blue suited middle-aged man seated to the convener's left lit and puffed a Cuban cigar to red-tipped glowing life. "But there is hope for the next election. Rumour has it Evan Reid will stay for the transition and resign before the end of next year."

"And Deputy Prime Minister Mendez will be on the way back to her family and business in Vancouver before the signature ink dries on his letter of resignation." The logo and print on the golf shirt worn by the younger man on the convener's right labeled him a member of Ottawa's most exclusive club.

The convener lifted and tilted the decanter over the three empty snifters. Amber liquor darkened the stoutly set bottom-heavy bells. "If the rumours prove true, this begs the question of whom the Liberals will chose to lead their party. There does not appear to be a strong contender in the prime minister's cabinet, definitely no one with his cachet."

The fourth man seated across the table crossed his legs and pinched the crease at the knee of his black suit pants. "The House leader has been mentioned."

The lone smoker snuffed out his cigar. "Bashir is too young. That fact aside, do you really believe Canada is ready to accept and embrace a Muslim as the leader of their government? I think not."

The convener finished his brandy and poured another. "The question we must answer is who will lead us when we respectfully request that our current rather tepid party leader step down after October's anticipated trouncing. While I anticipate several candidates will put her and his hand up, we must not risk squandering the opportunity to rebuild and take back Parliament once Reid is gone." The senior parliamentarian with five successful campaigns to his riding re-election credit cradled the snifter in both of his hands. He leaned forward on elbows rested at his knees and stared into the eyes of the man across the table. Eyes magnified by thick lenses. "We've asked you twice and twice you've backed away. This is your time. We won't ask again."

The fourth man ran long, thin fingers through his slicked-back, precision-cut black hair and shoved black rimmed glasses up the bridge of his nose. He smiled and lifted his glass. "How can I refuse your most generous and humbling vote of confidence? I would be honoured to lead the Conservative Party."

The four men raised snifters of spirits in a show of committed solidarity. "Gentlemen, I propose a toast." The convening party president stood. "To the next Tory Prime Minister of Canada Kingston Poirier."

Delicate crystal clinked and chimed in unified salute.

THE END

Acknowledgements

This story wrote itself once this storyteller let the characters take over.

The mystery I'd plotted didn't fit the Type A personalities of Jeri-lynn Connor and Alec Martin. Prime Minister Evan Reid's conflict, regret and need to keep a final promise shifted the theme political and the genre toward intrigue.

Credit for the snap in *Capital Strings* goes to my editor Sidney Blake. Her constructive critique challenges me to do better.

Thank you to Quebecer friend and author Trixie White for correcting my French, copy editor Lucinda Resnick for combing through the manuscript from first draft to layout, and my team of advisors and advance review copy readers on either side of the border.

My partner in love and life listens as I read what's been written, asks the questions I need to answer, and prompts me to continue when the words aren't quite right. Merci, John. Je t'aime.